MINE TO DEFY

JANEAL FALOR

Mine to Defy © 2021 Janeal Falor
ISBN-13 for Print Book: 978-1-946860-09-5
Cover Designed by MiblArt
To learn more about this author, please visit: janealfalor.com

❀ Created with Vellum

CHAPTER 1

My bald head and the ink tattooed across my face were the outward signs I was different than before I left home. That my disfigurement included barrenness was something I still didn't want to process.

The crowd amassed at the castle gawked in the direction of the motorcar I was in. The electric lights on lampposts flickered next to the castle doorway, while the spelled sparkling lights lit up the stone path.

The day I'd dreaded for over a year was here—today I returned home to the royal court as a tarnished.

In the country I just came from, Chardonia, people considered less than shadows were taken, and spelled to become bald and barren. Their faces were inked, and they were called *tarnished*. It was what I'd become, instead of the perfect member of the royal family I had been.

"Princess Tawny, your parents are waiting." The man who escorted me from the border wanted me out of the motorcar.

I held back a disdainful glare—easy enough to do with my royal training—and braced myself to leave the fake safety of the backseat, while avoiding the gazes of all those staring at me. I didn't want to see the disgust—or worse, pity—in their eyes. They

1

murmured, but I couldn't make out any of their bitter words through the open window.

My thoughts strayed to my parents. The queen would be happy to see me, but not in the state I was in. It was one reason I'd avoided coming home for so long. That and the Chardonians, our neighboring kingdom, had needed my help, but only for less than a year. After that I could have stayed, but they didn't need me. I didn't want to find my new place in society, but my place hurtled toward me, whether I wanted it to or not.

As I stepped out, a collective gasp was followed by a rustle of whispers, harsh against my ears. It'd been the same when I tried to cross the border into the country, except guards had stopped me then. Only the ring with the royal seal on it got me through. Thank the queen I'd had the foresight to ask my parents to send it.

I walked forward, and the crowd's exclamations increased, not so much that I could make out what they were saying, but enough to know they were shocked by what they saw. The perfect princess was gone, replaced by someone who resembled a refugee. Most escapees from Chardonia, the country just to the east of us, were tarnished.

I was past wishing I could spell my way out of this. I entered the castle set in the low mountains, and the doors closing behind me cut off the onlookers. To my horror, the servants lined up along the hall in honor of my return. More stares followed as I went, a freak among the pristine white walls and floors.

Zipping past them with pricks of discomfort hot across my face, I hurried through halls I'd once forgotten but that now came back in a rush of familiarity. Magic was everywhere—in the paintings, the warmth of the room, the fragrance of wildflowers. Home was like it had always been.

I was the thing that had changed.

All around me was light and airy. The castle was the opposite of everything dark and oppressive that had become my life.

I shook away the thought and stopped in front of the door to my mother's sitting room, where my parents waited for me. As a servant opened the door and announced my arrival, my insides quaked. The king and queen might not accept me now that I was so different, despite having the royal ring and being their daughter.

I wanted to run back to Chardonia and bury myself in helping others. Their cruel leaders were no longer in power, and I wanted the company of my friends who were back in the country that no longer needed me. But training kicked in. I held my head high, despite the shame inked across my face and the shine that had to be on my bald head, and urged myself forward.

I saw my mother first. The queen of Envado sat regally as ever —makeup, dress, and hair spelled to shimmer a light gold, highlighting the darkness of her black hair. Age had tried to gray it before I left, but she'd magicked it. Word had reached me that her usual flash and glam dissipated when I went missing while aiding those who needed it in Chardonia, but she appeared the same as ever to me.

My father was less stately, sitting back with only a hint of gold shimmering through his suit. His hair had gone silver. He never dyed it, much to my mother's chagrin. His steel-gray eyes softened as they met mine. I hurried to look back at Mother, not wanting to see his response to the degradation I'd gone through in forcibly becoming a tarnished.

I dipped into a curtsy. I should have taken the maid's offer this morning to find me something more suitable to wear to meet my royal parents. Uncertain how they'd react to my changed state, I kept my tone formal. "Mother. Dad. A pleasure to see you again."

"None of that, Tawny." The skin around Mother's eyes as she took in my state was tight. I'd like to blame the clothes, but it was my face her gaze lingered on. Despite that tightness, there was a relief in her eyes and a subtle lessening of tension around her mouth the longer she looked at me. From her, it was a great show of emotion. "We've missed you. Come hug me," she said.

Grateful to be in their presence again, I moved closer, but Dad was already out of his chair, to meet me partway with a hug. His embrace enveloped me in warm memories of my innocent youth.

"Daddy." The whispered word spilled out of me before I could stop it, but I didn't care.

"My girl." Was he crying?

The king never cried.

"I'm here now. Everything will be fine." It was a lie I told him and me both.

"Now Ridger, don't monopolize her." Mother's voice cracked. She might not like how I looked, but she had still missed me.

I gave Dad's arm a squeeze and slipped from his embrace. My mother hadn't left her chair by the fire, despite seeming so eager to see me. I hurried over to her, grateful she met my gaze this time without a crack in her façade. My dad breaking down was one thing, my mother quite another.

When we pulled apart, she cleared her throat and straightened her dress.

"Your siblings will be happy to see you when they rejoin us in a week's time. They're out on matters of state," she said, with a grin.

I barely knew my two older brothers. They were always gone, doing one thing or another. "It's fine."

The room grew awkwardly quiet, Dad standing near me and Mother still in her chair.

After a moment's silence, she sniffed and said, "Yes, well, we're glad you've returned to us. I only wish…" Her gaze glided to the top of my head.

My cheeks burned, and I turned away before she could see the humiliation rushing through me. They'd known I was a tarnished —the whole country had—but it was a fact that still shocked everyone. I would never again be or look like the carefree princess they'd all known before I left.

"Things will be put right again, now that you're home and we can… cover up your misfortunes."

Cover up who I'd become, she meant. I couldn't handle any more hiding. "It's been a long journey. I'd like to retire to my room."

4

"Yes, dear. Refresh yourself, and then join us for dinner. It will be wonderful to have you at the table again," my mother said, flicking a piece of lint from her skirt.

I didn't look at her again, as I dipped into a curtsy and rushed from the room. It took me a moment to realize my dad remained at my side.

"I would like to escort you to your new room, if you're willing," he said.

Comfort filled my chest. I wished I was a child again, so he could read to me like he used to.

It was a full second later before I realized what he'd said. "My *new* room? What happened to my old one?" I asked.

"There's some of that spunk in your gaze I've missed." He sighed. "The queen thought that part of the castle should be refurbished to accommodate guests. She has moved your room back to the royal wing."

I harrumphed. There was a reason I begged to have my room moved when I was eleven, and it was only emphasized by her moving it back. Not even a sense of freedom in the royal wing. At least I'd be away from the prying eyes of others who sometimes visited the east wing.

We wound our way in silence, passing servants who bowed and guards who kept attentive to their duty. It was a relief when we finally crossed over into the royal wing, past the last of the guards, and saw no one.

Until Dad said, "Don't hide it from me, like you did in your letters. How bad was it?"

I cringed. I'd sent letters after Chardonia's ruler was dead and I'd been free again, about six or seven months ago. I'd tried to keep things easier for them when I'd written, but he would see through my attempts. "It's better now."

"But before...?"

Before I came to terms with being tarnished, he meant. When I was captured and made into what I now was and forced into servitude. Stopping, I stared into his eyes. "I'd rather not talk about it."

He looked me over for a long moment, before finally conceding. "I had Mila decorate your room when we moved it."

"You know me well." My lady's maid and sometimes guard would know my tastes better than anyone. But as we came to my door and he opened it for me, it hit me just how much I didn't have the same preferences I used to.

The room glowed a soft pink, which meant whoever cast the spell had to keep their emotions steady while doing so. Whatever the emotions a person felt affected the color of the spell. Not every color was the same for every person and they could change over time, but if you knew yourself and had control, this wouldn't have been too difficult, just time-consuming.

It smelled faintly of wildflowers, and flowers made of magical light scattered all over the room gleamed with different colors. The caster had to feel a different emotion for each color of flower. It was a lot of work. The walls glimmered like massive jewel-toned diamonds, catching the light. And those were only the spells I made out on first glance. The mass of magic and gaudiness fluttering through the room made me want to throw something.

Had I really been so vain, to want nothing but spells like the attention-grabbing mass here?

"The slump of your shoulders tells me you're not pleased," Father said.

"I'm sorry. I don't mean to be a hassle, but I've changed a lot since I left Envado."

His gaze was intense on my face, probably him taking in my tarnished state, something I'd never be able to forget. He said, "I wish it wasn't so, Tawny."

Leaving to assist those under an oppressive rule was the right thing to do, but becoming tarnished? It left me cold. "That makes two of us."

CHAPTER 2

A week back at the castle and things weren't going smoothly. Oh, I attended meals and acted like I should, but Mother remained aloof, and many of the servants stared at me from the corners of their eyes.

I didn't leave my rooms much, but at least my dad was kind. He often visited me, taking the time with me that my mother never seemed to have. *Too many affairs of state* was her excuse, but that hadn't stopped her before I left for Chardonia. When I did get a chance to see her, she was still warm, if a bit stiff.

I had come to terms with the fact that I was different than before. Or at least I thought I did. Coming back here, with everyone either staring at me or avoiding looking my way, was a different story. It left my skin, especially on my head, itching. Things had definitely been easier among the other tarnished and the Chardonians—but they needed me no longer. Besides, my parents had been begging for me to come back.

Tonight, a celebration ball for my return was to take place. Mother had probably planned it before she saw my face. Yes, she knew I was a tarnished before I came home, and she understood what that meant, but hearing about it and seeing it were two different things.

7

I was expected to attend the ball as the guest of honor, but no one in Envado would want to see a bald, tattoo-faced princess. I heaved out a breath.

"Heavy sigh, Princess," Mila said from the corner of the room where she was arranging my dress. She, at least, talked to me like she had before I left, even if she wouldn't look me in the face.

"I'm fine. What dress did my mother pick out for tonight?" I turned away from the window to see what she'd set out.

The sight that met my eyes had me holding in a shudder. The dress flashed from one color to the next, covering the spectrum of the rainbow. It sparkled brightly. It was flamboyant, calling far more attention than I felt comfortable with. The cut itself wasn't terrible, but the skirt was large enough it'd get in the way of the dancing that'd be required of me. Assuming Mother could cajole anyone into dancing with the damaged princess.

No. If I had to go to the ball, I wasn't going to do it in this monstrosity. "Thank you for following orders, Mila, but my tastes are different now."

Her smile widened into the first real grin I'd seen from her since my arrival. "Yes, Princess."

She fluttered away with that dress and stashed it in the wardrobe we used to call *the dumpster*. As she whirled around, she asked, "What did you have in mind instead?" She met my gaze for a brief moment, before it skirted away.

I'd almost felt normal, conspiring to wear something other than what my mother wished, but it didn't make up for the fact that everything was different. I was no longer who I once was, and I didn't know how court would react to that. I cleared my throat. "That white dress I brought home with me? A friend made it for me. If we put some subtle spells on it, it'll be more to my liking."

She raised an eyebrow, like she had the first time she came in my rooms when I'd asked her to take down all the spells she'd cast, but she'd gotten to work and fixed them. "This one?" She pulled the sleek white dress out from my main wardrobe.

8

It almost shimmered in the fading light of day coming in from my window. The fabric was thin compared to the other one. Delicate. Something I'd never been, but that felt far better suited to my personality now, and to how I wanted to face the court upon my return. "That's the one," I said. "Let's spell it like it has a shimmer as it does in the sunlight—subtle but there."

"And what else?" she asked, eyeing the dress.

"That's it."

Her other eyebrow rose. "If you're certain, it'll be but a moment."

Leaving her to it, I turned toward the mirror over the dresser. It was ornate, like everything else in my room, but spells no longer danced across the intricate carvings in the wooden frame. I usually avoided looking in the mirror, but it couldn't be avoided today.

My bald head stood out, as Mila's long locks slipped down her back behind me in the reflection. The tattooed lines woven across my face made my head where my hair should have been appear dull in comparison. I didn't know if I wanted to hide them even if I could. I'd taught others in Chardonia to be proud of their tattoos; it seemed wrong to turn my own nose up at them.

Across the dresser were paint pots full of all sorts of shades near my skin color I was certain were to cover my tattoos. Next to them, a thick, long wig hung on a mannequin's head, waiting to hide my baldness.

I scowled at it.

It would be easy to cover up what had happened to me, but it would be like erasing all that had happened instead of learning from it.

Mila glided over to me, the dress draped across her arm. "Here you go, Princess. Would you like me to help you with your makeup?"

It was the first she'd offered since I came home. Clothes, hair, and makeup used to be our favorite things to do together, besides casting spells.

9

I didn't try to hide the longing from my voice when I said, "I'm not sure I want to hide the tattoos."

"Oh?"

I was thankful she didn't pry more, but did add, "They're a part of who I am now. Besides, my hair won't ever grow back. I've had healers look at it, and the damage is so great, there's nothing that can be done to fix it. There's nothing left to grow from. The tattoos are the same. If they were normal tattoos, someone could remove them, but the magic used to create them was strong and no one knows how to counter it." Magic could change them, but I didn't know anyone who'd figured out how to mask them, and I wasn't certain I wanted to anyway.

I shivered at the thought of the depraver who did this to me, but quickly shoved him from my mind.

"Well, then, we could highlight your eyes if you'd like. Bring them out," Mila said.

I stared at myself. There wasn't anything that would detract from my tattoos. Yet, it would make her feel better. "If you'd like."

She got to work, and soon I was dolled up and ready for the ball. The makeup was kept light, far too tasteful for current fashions, but I liked it.

The dress shimmered as it clung to me. It moved with me so I could breathe and dance, but best of all, it had pockets. Katherine, the woman from Chardonia who'd sent me home with clothes befitting my station, was a gem. She worked magic with clothes, and had made some especially for me. Thinking of her made my heart twist for her and my friends. It was lonely here.

No sense, putting it off any longer. Mother would have a fit that I was late, but this way, she wouldn't be able to make me change before the ball.

After giving Mila my thanks and dismissing her for the night, I headed out. She wouldn't need to guard me, when so many others were on duty for the evening.

Other than some guards standing at attention along the way, the corridor was empty of people until I reached the royal waiting room. That was where we waited, as a family, until my mother deemed it time to enter. The royal family had to make a big entrance once everyone arrived.

"Tawny, why aren't you wearing the dress I sent? It's the latest fashion. Nothing like that gown." The first words out of my mother's mouth stung.

I straightened, despite wanting to curl in on myself. "Just changing things to fit my own style, like I always have."

"Yes, dear, but now you stand out too much. You should do something to temper that."

Her statement was delivered kindly, but the underlying blade found my heart all the same. I would never fit in again.

I swallowed down my fear and loneliness. I'd stand out, no matter what she did to force me to be like everyone else.

Before I could retort, Dad was at my side. "Leave her be, Brundy. This is a celebration for her. Let's remember that and enjoy that she's returned to us."

She sniffed, her dress flashing between a fuchsia and a bright violet that would have gone well with the dress she'd picked for me. "Very well."

Once she'd turned toward the door and directed the servants to announce us, I gave my dad a grateful smile, though I feared it was soured by my feelings.

He leaned over and whispered, 'We'll get through this night together."

I'd never thought about how my dad had managed through these nights before, but it made sense that he'd struggled through them. Mother was always the center of attention, leaving him on the outskirts. I'd been too wrapped up in myself to realize it, but memories of him alone on his throne or waiting alone in a room full of people came to me. Maybe I could find someone to fit in with.

The doors opened, and Mother strode forward, Dad following at my side. The people stared as I came in. The flash of colors, sparkles, and fireworks spelled across the room made me want to cringe.

Instead, I took my place on my throne to the left side of my mother, sitting with my back straight.

I looked over the crowd of witches and warlocks, wishing I could be anywhere but here. My mother's voice was muffled in my ears and no one gazed at her. The entirety of court seemed to be here, and more.

A pair of wildly brown eyes stood out to me, but they got lost so fast in the mass, I wasn't certain they'd been there to begin with.

Alone in a sea of familiar and unfamiliar faces, I couldn't wait for the night to be over.

CHAPTER 3

I'd last been to a ball shortly before I left for Chardonia. It should have been clear then that my life would never be the same, but as those things go, I didn't have any idea what I was getting myself into. I'd been the princess, but I was also a courtier amongst many other courtiers. Now, I stood out. Not only because of my tarnished state, but also because of the outfit I'd chosen. Between not being colored and barely being spelled, my dress stood out against everyone else's.

Perhaps Mother's choice would have been better, but at least this wasn't overly gaudy.

Dad walked over to me and held out a hand. "Shall we?"

I didn't want to dance, but he was trying to be gallant and please everyone, like he always did. "Thank you," I said.

He swirled me around the floor, the other guests staying far from us with long looks and whispers. Instead of focusing on them, I looked up at my dad. He still looked youthful, despite the gray hair. There was something happy about his eyes.

"Thank you for the dance." I wanted to add, *despite my being the least desirable partner in the room*, but I held my tongue.

"You're welcome."

When the song ended with a flourish of colored, magical lights

13

moving to the music and then crackling like fireworks, a courtier claimed my father.

Father asked me, "Would you like me to escort you back to the throne?"

"I'm fine. You do what the king must."

With a grateful smile, he turned to the woman, and I turned back toward my throne. I strode toward it, focusing on getting there. Before, I would have been stopped and asked to dance or share my thoughts on a subject, or I'd be admired for a spell I cast. Now, there was a wide berth around me.

"Princess, may I have your hand for the next dance?" a young man asked.

I turned around to face him, as he held out a hand with a slight bow, his gaze everywhere but on me. He was impeccably dressed and traditionally handsome, exactly the sort of man my mother would want me to court.

"Did the queen put you up to this?" Because I couldn't imagine he did it on his own, unless it was a dare.

His cheeks reddened.

I sighed. "I'm going to the punch bowl. You can find the woman you actually wish to dance with."

A relieved expression flashed on his face, before his courtier mask was back in place. "Let me at least guide you to it." He held out his arm, which I begrudgingly took.

The room parted for us—as if I needed more proof that everyone was aware of my movements—and murmurs followed us.

"Do you see the shine on her head?"

"Look at those markings."

"*Tsk.* She used to be such a beauty."

I didn't bother paying attention to the others. The cuts were still raw.

I let go of the man escorting me when we were still steps away from the refreshment table. He hurried away like I had something contagious.

Disgusted, I pursed my lips to keep from saying something my mother would be embarrassed about. I took a punch cup from a server with a murmured *thank you,* and headed down the row, taking in more of the space.

The ballroom was vast and filled to the brim with dancers. Scattered groups of people were talking here and there, but mostly guests liked to see and be seen. The spells they'd spent so much money on or so much time cultivating had to be shown off. Their wealth and prestige were more than I could stand, when they were flaunted so wholly by people looking down their noses on anyone different.

I scoffed.

"I agree completely," a male voice said from my right.

I strolled away as casually as I could. I wanted to run from the room but instead, I came to a stop in a corner near a potted plant, watching the crowd but not my sides.

Someone had snuck up on me. He said, "Hello."

Surprise loosened my tongue. "You dare speak with the outcast?"

"Actually, I wanted to have a conversation with you."

At this, I turned, to see what man would pay any heed to the scorned princess. The wildly brown eyes I'd caught in the crowd before stood out. Their depths spoke of deep conviction and adventure that took my breath away.

Once I forced myself to look past those eyes, it was a pleasant surprise to find a handsome, but not classically so, man was paying attention to me. His nose was a smidgen too big, and his mouth a bit too small to be considered kissable, but he was still an attractive young man about my age of nineteen, perhaps a couple years older.

I jerked my attention back to the ball, without paying attention to anything else about him, and set my cup on a passing servant's tray. "Why would you wish to speak with me?"

"Can't a man wish to know the most interesting woman in the room?"

That was me all right—interesting. "No," I said.

"I confess, that response is not what I expected."

I flashed him a glare. Might as well be my charmingly blunt self. "Why don't you see what everyone else here does? I'm different, the kind you don't want to be associated with."

"But I'd like to—"

"Go away." I didn't feel like dealing with someone who only meant to brag to his friends that he'd spoken with the tarnished princess. I couldn't see any other reason he would be here.

"Lonvar Dastik," he said. "I'm happy to make your acquaintance."

"Wonderful," I murmured, though it wasn't.

Before he could react, the heralds announced the newcomers.

The men swept into the room with all their gleaming, too-bright smiles and blue suits with dazzling spells sparkling off them. The younger brother's grin wasn't as wide and he held back more, always a bit shyer, but still backing my oldest brother up when he needed something. The older one let out a burst of rainbow spells, skillfully mastering what emotion he felt to rapidly change the colors. Those gathered, visibly buoyed by the new arrivals, crowded forward. I slunk back against the wall. *Brothers.*

"Does the princess not care to greet her brothers? I understand they've been gone for some time, and you've only just returned yourself." Lonvar brought my attention back to him. I took the time to look closer at him; his suit was not as fancy as many of the tuxes here, and while it was spelled to have a sheen to it, there weren't many outfits that had less magic placed upon them. Something about it had me wanting to open up to him, at least a little.

There was no love lost between us siblings. We didn't have a chance to be close before I left, and I wasn't about to change that. No, I couldn't tell him anything. "You can leave now."

He studied me, giving me the impression he was about to go,

when someone tumbled into him from behind and sent him my way.

Lonvar caught himself on the wall before he rammed into me.

The woman in a soft pink gown who'd jostled him gave a slurred *sorry* and stumbled off, to get closer to my brothers.

I scoffed, and Lonvar gave me a quizzical glance.

"It's ridiculous." I found myself wanting to explain how I felt to *someone*, as the woman left. I usually talked a lot more at these events, but now no one except Dad wanted to listen. Lonvar wasn't my first choice, but he was my only one. "All of Envado is full of people tripping over themselves to get to my brothers or the next great spell. None of them care about the world around us."

He surprised me by moving closer. "But you do." His voice was soft against the laughter of the crowd at some antics my brothers were up to.

"And look where it got me." The bitter words ripped out of me.

Instead of turning away and toward the more acceptable members of my family, he held out a hand. "Dance with me?"

My first instinct was to question why and fight against it, but I used to love to dance. His invitation held none of the sense of obligation—familial or enforced—my father's and the other young man's did. This seemed to be neither of those.

My hand moved of its own accord, as the tension building behind my eyes lessened. "No one else is dancing."

Lonvar led me to the half of the ballroom where couples had come together earlier and which was now bare, since everyone vied for the chance to close in on the crown prince and his quiet brother.

At least no one would be staring at the spectacle Lonvar was about to make of himself. Not that I cared.

A song already played, fainter than it'd been before, the spell amplifying it having ceased so people could better hear whatever story my brothers told. Still, the lively melody tickled the soles of my feet clad in white flats. It was a traditional dance I'd grown up learning with my dad.

Lonvar held my right hand in his left one and put his other arm around me. His warmth startled me, but there was no time to think on it. We moved to the rhythm.

My feet barely touched the floor as we flew across the room, almost like the time I'd danced with magic lifting me. Now there was no magic—at least none I could detect.

Lonvar could dance. He led me this way and that, twirling and gliding across the floor. The noise around us faded and it was just him, me, and the music.

As my breaths came in winded gasps, a leap of delight shot through me. I couldn't remember the last time I felt so good. So normal. We spun across the room, and for the first time since leaving Chardonia, I belonged right where I was. I didn't know him, but it didn't matter. We moved together, as if we'd practiced every day, our entire lives.

I stared into his eyes, his gaze intense upon me. My cheeks flushed. I didn't know if it was his stare or the music. When the song neared its close, he pulled me close and dipped me back.

The room was utterly silent as I straightened. Everyone behind him had turned their attention away from my brothers, to watch us. Both my brothers scowled down at us from their vantage point on the dais, arms crossed over their chests. Mother's expression was politically polite, giving away nothing, but Dad beamed at me. It was his smile that undid me.

I came to myself, the room blaring in its quiet. I'd made a spectacle of myself, it would seem, with a man I didn't know. I moved to pull away from him, but his hand gripped me tight.

Angry memories of being held by the depravers flooded me. The lead depraver inching toward me with hungry eyes that wanted to burn and damage me, a prisoner from a lost battle against the Grand Chancellor. The depraver's teeth shined in the harsh light, already finding joy in my fear.

I ripped my thoughts back to the present and my hand from

his. I slipped it deep into my pocket. Thankfully, I had enough presence of mind to not storm away and invite more gossip, but I couldn't stop myself from glaring at him, either.

To his credit, Lonvar remained unruffled. "Thank you for the dance, Princess." He bowed. "Would you like some more refreshment?"

I wanted to scream at him, for trying to keep me close. It wasn't really him I was angry at. The bitter emotions were all for me and the depraver who tarnished me. The depraver had been rounded up with the others and those previous rulers of Chardonia, the ones who had done such hateful, terrible things. Dehumanizing whoever got in their way and treating women as a commodity of magic instead of the people they were. The leaders were all either dead or imprisoned. There was no one left to be angry at.

Instead of voicing all this, I merely nodded, but my jaw was tight with tension.

He offered his arm, but I didn't take it. I headed toward the punch bowl once again, relieved to be back under my own control. What happened during that dance? I was almost like the old Tawny.

We were served sparkling punch, spelled to taste like our most desired drink, but I didn't sip mine. Thoughts of what to say to Lonvar tumbled about in my head, awkward and uncomfortable.

"How do you like the weather?" I asked.

"Don't stop being the woman I danced with. She was anything but demure." He gave an impish wink.

Internally, I laughed. Outwardly, I gave a placid smile. I wasn't ready to show him more of the real me. "What is it that brought you to the ball this evening?"

Before he got the chance to respond, the crowd descended upon us, led by my brothers.

Rumam, my eldest brother and the crown prince, reached us first. The grin on his face was jovial as ever, but the glare he gave Lonvar was not. "Who's the bloke?"

"The *bloke* is Lonvar Dastik," Lonvar replied firmly.

He stood up for himself. I liked that. It made my own mouth move. "He's quite the gentleman," I said.

"Is that so?" Rumam asked. "And what does this *Lonvar* think he's doing with my sister?"

I didn't bother keeping back my eye roll. It was bad enough he and Herni never paid much mind to me. Worse that they now were. I couldn't say if it was because I'd danced with Lonvar or because I'd caught the attention of the crowd they'd been working. They'd never cared when I danced with men before I left for Chardonia.

"Just dancing." Lonvar scooted closer to me, with the people pressing in, and took the opportunity to whisper in my ear, "I'd like a chance to get to know you better."

The suggestion startled me, but I didn't let it show. I said, "Dear brothers, let's talk about how you've been the past couple of years."

"Better than you." Though mumbled under his breath, Rumam's words hit me like shards of ice, cold and sharp.

He kept speaking, my other brother nodding in the background, but the rush in my ears didn't allow me to hear what he said. The unspoken had been spoken. As a family that'd always hid the darker things, mine were just laid bare. I wanted nothing further to do with my brothers.

CHAPTER 4

The ball started back up when Rumam said, "Where's the dancing?"

The musicians played, their instruments spelled to enhance the music. My brothers each took a young woman out onto the dance floor, and everyone else coupled up and followed their lead.

Everyone, that was, but Lonvar.

I sipped my drink, which tasted like refreshing water but sat heavy in my stomach. "You don't have to stay."

"Your brothers are foolish to treat you in such a fashion."

I gave him a sharp look. "Don't let them or my mother hear you say that."

"Fair point." He raised his glass to his lips. "But that doesn't make me wrong."

I stared at him as he drank. What sort of man dared speak like that? "It makes you insane," I said.

He went on, as if nothing concerned him. "I understand your parents and brothers, but I meant what I said before. I'd like to get to know you better. Perhaps a drive through the countryside, tomorrow afternoon? My motorcar isn't the latest model like most here would have, but it's spelled to keep the cold air out."

"Why would you want to get to know me?" It was a forward question for a ball where people usually didn't say directly what they meant, but he appeared to be the type I could be forward with, and I truly wanted to understand.

He looked to those dancing. "You seem like a person worth knowing."

"Because I'm a tarnished princess?" I didn't want to play the part of a jester.

"Because you are a woman with an inner fire I'd like to understand." His gaze found mine again. He must have seen my hesitation, because he added, "And a back seat for a chaperone, of course."

I stuck out my chin. "I'm far past needing a chaperone, with the things I've seen." Horrors of others who'd been forced to become tarnished and become slaves for men who flaunted their power before us and the women they controlled. The abuse, physically and emotionally, still echoed across my skin and ears. My own trials were exhausting to live through, but seeing others go through it had been devastating.

Despite all that, I'd made it out after the Grand Chancellor had been defeated and the balance of the government shifted. Some of my friends were a part of that new government. Good changes had come because of my friends. I had also taken the time to lift others who'd been damaged both outwardly and emotionally under the Grand Chancellor's rule. A little time spent with a man my age would be nothing compared to all that. Especially with Mila at my back as my guard.

His eyes darkened, and though his voice was strained, he kept his words light. "It's your choice."

Rumam laughed brashly at something his dance partner said. I didn't have to look over, to know I wouldn't want to be in the castle when everyone woke up and have to deal with another day of royal monotony. Besides, I'd done nothing but stay in here since my return. I couldn't hide forever, and I certainly had no desire to. Lonvar might not be my first choice, I'd rather be alone, but it was the break I needed.

"The front steps at one," I said.

MILA and I didn't exactly sneak out, since most of the castle's residents except the servants were still in bed, but I didn't make my plans known to most, either. Guilt ebbed and flowed, depending on whom I considered telling. I let my dad know, last night. He raised an eyebrow but didn't say anything about it, except to insist I take a guard.

Shortly after midnight last night, Dad escorted me back to my room with words of encouragement about the ball and my brothers, but I didn't believe him.

As I slipped through the halls and down toward the entrance now, my heart beat faster. It wasn't sneaking out. I was of age, and more than that, I'd been on my own long enough that I didn't want to report to anyone again. Dad knew, and Mila was with me. That was enough.

A servant opened the door for us, and I headed down the stairs as an old-styled motorcar pulled up. The motor was encased in a color that appeared silver and looked newly washed and shiny, despite its age. The black tires matched the paint, no glass in the windows, or they were rolled down, except for the front windshield. From where I was, the dark leather seats looked worn and cracked with age but appeared comfortable.

Lonvar jumped out. He flashed a grin my way, flicking his gaze at something behind me. I glanced where he looked, but saw nothing except the closed door. When I turned my attention to him, he watched me with a careful expression. "Afternoon, Princess." He held the door open for me.

"You don't have to call me that."

"Of course, I do."

I ignored this and said, "This is Mila, my lady's maid." No sense in telling him she was as well trained at defending me as I was. He didn't seem to be a threat, but one never knew.

He dipped his head toward her. "Pleasure."

She waved a hand. "Please, pretend like I'm not here. You two have a nice drive."

A flush of heat spread across my skin. I hadn't expected her to say that, but it was a nice thought. I couldn't forget she was here. If I did, I'd demand that he return me to the castle at once. I wouldn't let my guard down completely with this stranger even if I did feel a pull to be with him. Probably because he was attractive in his own right.

He didn't say anything about my breeches, but then again, many women wore them here. Mine were black and unspelled, though, unlike most other Envadi's would be. Even for a day trip, there should be something magical about my clothes. My flowing blue blouse was likewise magic free and suited me.

He surprised me by not having any spells on his attire either. His motorcar was a different story, as I climbed into it and felt the temperature regulated to make me perfectly comfortable. Why did he have so many blankets in the back seat, next to Mila, then? Suspicion turned the moment that could have been freedom sour. He appeared to be poor, at least more so than most of court, and was trying to charm me. Did he want to use me as a means to become royal himself, or something more?

I wanted to like him, but I didn't trust him. This was just a way to get out from the castle and enjoy some time without the expectations of court. I had Mila and my own powers. The two of us would keep me safe.

After closing my door, he strode to the other side and scooted in. Soon, the motorcar was merrily chugging away from my childhood home and to the open road. None of us spoke as we drove through the city. Many people were out, but without the royal flags and procession, no one paid us any particular mind. If someone happened to look inside the motorcar, I appeared to be just another tarnished refugee from Chardonia.

I relaxed into my seat, enjoying the light bounce beneath me. More so when we got out of the city, and Lonvar sped up. I inhaled deeply, wishing I could smell the fresh air, and gave a grin.

"You like a little speed in your life, I see," he said after a while.

I looked out the windshield at the trees blurring by, as we climbed farther up the mountains in which the capitol rested. "You have caught me, sir."

"Is going for a fast drive all it takes, to get on your good side?"

I laughed, not caring that I was opening myself up to him more than anyone in Envado besides my dad and Mila. The drive was making me drunk on freedom I hadn't felt since I'd become tarnished. "The speed helps." The distance from the heaviness of expectations, more so.

"I see." And from the way he looked at me, it felt like he heard my thoughts.

"Keep your eyes on the road." I couldn't bring myself to put a bite in my words. It had been a long time since someone looked at me and not at the baldness and tattoos.

Though he turned back toward the road, there was a hint of a smile on his lips. He slowed the motorcar. "How about some fresh air?"

I cocked my head. "You mean...?"

"Getting rid of the spells, feeling the cold air on our faces, and enjoying the warmth of a blanket."

It sounded more than lovely. "I'm for it." With a flick of his hand, a soft-green spell with a hint of pink swirls hit the spells surrounding the car. The temperature immediately dropped, but with it, the breath of fresh mountain air I yearned for entered, full of trees and spice.

I reached back and Mila gave me two blankets, keeping a couple for herself. I handed him one and tucked another around myself, grateful there was plenty of space between us. I might have been getting cozy, but that didn't mean I wanted to cozy up to him.

By the time I looked back at him, he was settled with the

blanket on his lap and draped loose over his legs, so he could still maneuver the motorcar. Mila had likewise huddled up but remained silent.

Knowing she was taking care of herself, but also watching the scene unfold, I decided to do what I could to get more information out of Lonvar. "Had this vehicle long?"

"It was my father's." He sounded sad.

I shouldn't pry, but— "*Was?*"

"He died."

I guessed as much. I wanted to ask more, but his tone was so closed off in those two words, I didn't want to push the issue. "Do you have any living family?"

"I'm an only child, but my mother's alive and well. She lives in a country house in the south."

"Wish I was an only child." Except then, I'd have to rule. I made a face.

"Siblings can be difficult."

I shook my head. "That, definitely, but also, it'd mean I'd be the heir. I'd rule if I had to, but I'm thankful there's someone else to do so. Especially now." Realizing I revealed more than I meant to, I hurried to add, "Besides, my brothers keep the queen occupied when I'd rather her attention not be on me."

"Your mother is close to them?" he asked.

"Yes and no. I don't think she can be close to anyone, but she has raised Rumam to rule in her stead. I don't think she wants to give up the throne anytime soon, though, since he's more inclined to travel and attend balls than focus on affairs of state."

"And the younger prince follows him everywhere?" Lonvar asked, glancing at me. When I raised my eyebrow, he shrugged and said, "Newspapers."

"Of course." When I left Chardonia, they'd been trying to get those started again for the populace as a whole, from verified sources, rather than only from the Grand Chancellor. "The papers probably know more about my brothers than I do."

"I see."

26

It felt like he understood far more than I said, but that didn't make me any less wary of him. I didn't know how he read my expressions and body language, when I'd been taught from such a young age to keep them carefully guarded, but he did.

"It's all a bit silly." I cleared my throat, awkwardness poking at me. "Oh, look. The dam."

The hydro-electric dam came into view as we rounded a corner. It provided electricity for the entire country.

"I haven't been up here in years," I said. "I know my brothers often come to events, up in the mountains, but I was never interested." The air grew chillier, and I pulled my blanket closer.

"Would you like me to put the spell back up?" he asked, his hand already raised.

"Please, no. It's much too lovely, even if it is cold."

"As you like." He grinned.

The crisp wind whipped across the air, adding a bite to it as we continued toward the dam. We raced past it and headed to a small, rough road.

Lonvar turned down it. He could be taking me anywhere.

Had I made a mistake, coming with him? I fisted my hand around part of the blanket. If he tried something, he'd find magic blasted at him faster than he knew how to handle things. Likely, by me and Mila both.

As we continued down, the bright green of the trees growing heavier, some of my tension lessened. The area was beautiful. It could be he was just taking us for a drive like he said. A bunny hopped off the dirt ahead, and I eased back. Seeing so much of the countryside was a pleasant change from the capital.

Lonvar pulled over to the side of the road and turned off the motorcar. I gripped the blanket more tightly, all my fears rushing back.

He said, "I thought we could go for a stroll."

"Here?" There wasn't much around—just trees, everywhere we looked. Then again, it was better than walking where other people could stare.

"Mila can come, of course."

That settled it. I wanted to stretch my legs, and she and I could take him if he tried anything. "Sounds perfect."

I hopped out of the motorcar, surprised that it wasn't as cold out as I expected. Now that the wind wasn't hitting me in the face at forty miles an hour, the temperature was more hike-able.

Though if I'd known we were going hiking, I'd have worn better shoes.

Lonvar slipped in between the trees, his steps silent. He was taking the lead, but it left me at his back, which was safer. I did the same to keep my steps quiet, keeping pace while watching him. I didn't want any surprises, but he seemed to only have enjoying nature on his mind. Still, I couldn't help the caution inching through me.

Mila was at our backs, and sure to have her hand on her gun or be ready with a spell.

The walk was nice, birds tweeting as we went. A squirrel crossed our path, delighting me despite the fact that I'd seen thousands of squirrels in my lifetime.

Was there anything I could do, to add to the area? Any spells that would help it along? I could pull nutrients from the ground around a plant and give them to the roots or do the same with water. The area looked healthy and thriving though. I only had so much magic, as everyone did, but it would build back up before I really needed it.

But with the color of spells giving away emotions, I wasn't ready to cast one in front of Lonvar just yet. Which emotions linked to which colors varied person to person, but because of certain generalities that occurred, someone well trained or who knew the caster well could pick up on some of the emotions coursing through them. I didn't want him to see what I felt, when I didn't know what it was myself.

We'd been walking perhaps twenty minutes, when I realized I was hearing something that didn't belong in nature. A mournful sound. Like a cry. A human calling out. I stopped.

Lonvar looked at me, eyes grave, and put a finger to his lips, catching both my gaze and Mila's. He crouched down and pointed to the left, down a hill. I took care of where I stepped, huddled next to him, and looked, Mila doing the same on my other side.

At first, I didn't understand what unfolded before me. People moved about between others huddled together. Someone shouted words I couldn't make out, but the angry undertone was clear. There was something odd about the group he yelled at. It pulled at me until it dawned on me. They were all bald and inked just like me.

Tarnished were being forced to the ground. One stood and the yeller backhanded them. We were in Envado, but the tarnished continued to be treated horribly.

CHAPTER 5

Fear gripped me, but so did determination to help them. And I was filled with questions.

Why did Lonvar bring me here? What were they doing with the tarnished? How did the tarnished come to be under their power? I would work on finding answers when there weren't dangers directly at hand.

"We have to get closer," I said.

Lonvar put a hand on my arm. "It's not safe."

Mila didn't say anything, but her gaze was focused on those below us.

My throat closed, my breath coming shallow as I ripped away from him. "You brought me here to join those down there as a captive, didn't you?"

Whipping her head toward him, Mila said, "I will kill you before that happens." Her hands were already aimed at him as she looked ready to spring herself at him.

Lonvar eyes widen with horror that I had to believe his next words. "I would never make another human a slave."

I looked him over a moment longer. I wanted to make certain my gut instinct to trust him was right, despite the warning in my mind to run away from anyone who dared try to hold me. I trusted him, with this at least. "I think he's telling the truth, Mila." And yet, I couldn't put off asking him any longer, "Why did you lead us here?"

He hesitated.

Mila didn't lower her arms, staying ready. It was on him if he made a wrong move.

"Tell us." My demand didn't seem nearly strong enough.

"I thought the one person in the royal family who would do something should know."

I studied his face intently but spotted no lies. Turning my attention back to the group below us, I asked, "What do you know?"

"Not as much as I want to. I do know they're keeping tarnished —both refugees and now some that they've kidnapped from Chardonia—for magic."

"Why would they need them for magic? And who would take it?" The previous Grand Chancellor of Chardonia had used the tarnished and the lower class as power sources for electricity, but with our hydro-electric dam, we had no such need in Envado. If we did, I'd use coal or go without before I used people. The kidnappers had to be sadists to do so.

"I'm not sure. If I knew that, maybe I'd know better how to counter them."

Taking in the scene playing out below us, I was grateful he'd shown me, even if I wished there was nothing to see happening in the first place. "I need a closer look."

"That's not a good idea," he said, at the same time as Mila said, "No."

I glared at him, knowing she wouldn't budge. "Why?"

"Because you look like them. Plus, you're third in line for the throne. If something happens to you, it'll be the country's loss and my head."

I thought the country would prefer something bad happening to me. I didn't want to risk Mila's position, but there were people that needed us. "I'm going in, anyway."

Before either could protest or grab me, I darted farther down the hill, careful to stay behind trees and bushes while keeping my steps. I got about halfway down, far closer to the people than I probably should, but I could make out what they said now, so I crouched behind a thick bush.

Lonvar and Mila came down beside me, the latter giving me a glare.

"Is this the last of them?" a man called out.

A woman rounded a copse of trees, something about her vaguely familiar.

I'd seen her before, her thick, shiny hair tickling my memories.

"Two more coming through," she said.

"We've got a good batch today. Should we start testing them?"

"Boss will do that later. We're just here to secure them." The woman headed back through the forest, away from us.

The man she'd been speaking with was one of ten people surrounding the area. There had to be between eighty and a hundred tarnished here. Tents were on the edges of the encampment. Each person lording over the tarnished had a gun at their waist and a hand on it, as if to counter any trouble. The tarnished had been so downtrodden, worth less than the shadows they cast. They wouldn't cause any trouble.

I couldn't say the same about me.

Unfortunately, I couldn't cause much trouble here and now without more help against the weapons, let alone without knowing how much magic the captors held.

The tarnished were gathered in small groups and tied to trees. There were about four to six in each group, and at least seven trunks being used. The tarnished were slumped as if in despair against the trees. A few appeared to be speaking to one another, but faintly and with wary glances at those who'd taken them.

The whole thing made my stomach flip.

Lonvar must have been worried, because he leaned over, his breath tickling my skin, and whispered in my ear, "We need to leave."

Mila placed a hand on my arm, as if she agreed.

I held up one finger, and studied those men and women holding the tarnished hostage. They would pay.

Satisfied I could remember each of the people who'd stood over the tarnished, I nodded back toward the hill, the way we'd come.

Relief shone in Lonvar's eyes, but he didn't relax.

Mila didn't let her relief show.

Lonvar motioned for me to go first. I threw one last look at the captives and saw that woman again—the one with the shiny, thick hair. I squinted at her, trying to place her, and took a step closer. A pop of cold air rushed by, and every kidnapper's head snapped in our direction. *An intruder spell.* I must have set it off.

"People, up the hill," a man called, pointing at us.

I didn't wait for Mila to hurry me on; I ran as fast as I could, but they had eyes on us. Guns went off, barging through the trees faster than we could run.

CHAPTER 6

I hurtled through the trees and bushes, staying low, as bullets whizzed past.

Lonvar was right beside me, darting in and out of trees but staying close.

Mila breathed heavily, almost on top of us.

We couldn't be captured. Someone had to remain free, to make sure these people were let go and their kidnappers brought to justice. More questions about Lonvar popped through my mind. How he knew to bring me here. Why he went to the ball.

Something nicked my right arm and stung. I didn't bother looking, with the amount of foliage whipping by. We had a head start, but while we wove through the trees trying not to be hit, we'd be visible in the open areas.

I wouldn't be captured again.

Would. Not.

I put on a burst of speed, and my legs ached as I ran up the hill. At least the same trees and bushes that got in our way would slow down our pursuers as well. Which gave me an idea. Without stopping, I swung my arm behind me and thrust out a spell. It flashed out of me in a torrent of yellow-muddied fear but bright with steely determination. The colors depicted my emotions so well,

34

but did the job of blasting a *whoosh* of air that would slow down our pursuers and give them something else to fight against.

As I ran I kept in mind they might send their own spells, along with their bullets. I knew from experience that Mila was sending out more spells to cover our backs. To defend me.

We reached the top of the hill but didn't stop. If anything, we went faster, tearing through the woods, dodging trees and jumping over bushes. I hadn't pushed myself this hard since I was training for battle in Chardonia. I should have never stopped.

My breathing grew harsher, as my sides ached.

Lonvar cast a spell too, covering up the way we came, then motioned for me to slow down. We went faster than walking pace, but not so much that we smashed through the woods. He was trying to conceal our location, and we were harder to find if we were silent and didn't leave any tracks.

The crashing and cursing from far behind us was loud, despite the distance. Glancing back, I saw nothing, but I wouldn't feel better until we were farther down the road.

Lonvar took my hand. I wanted to shake him off, but instead, let him lead me forward. I checked repeatedly, to make certain Mila stayed at our heels. Moments later, the motorcar came into view. I gave a silent thanks for its presence, and pushed myself the last bit. I scrambled to open the door, jumped in, and closed it quietly after me.

Mila hopped in, and Lonvar got in on his side. He started the engine, and we drove out in a rush of noise, after trying to be perfectly quiet.

I turned around, to see if anyone came after us, but no one was there. I whirled on Lonvar. "We left those tarnished behind. We have to do something."

"And end up captured, ourselves?"

"I can come back here with the army."

"It's not going to be that easy."

"Why ever not?"

Mila was silent in the back. When I checked on her, she was

more concerned with the road behind us than with anything going on up front.

Lonvar drummed his fingers across the steering wheel. "There's more than one place where this is happening. If we attack one spot and free the tarnished, the others will know we're on to them. They will find new places to go, and we'll be worse off than we are now."

"We'll make a coordinated attack."

"There are things you don't know." He growled, emanating frustration.

"Then tell me."

He didn't respond.

"Never mind," I said. "Why bring me here if you don't want me to do anything?"

"I needed you to see so you'd believe. I just… That is to say, I need…"

Clearly whatever it was would not come out easily. I didn't have time for his hesitation. "Tell me where all the locations are, and I'll deal with this."

"If only it was that easy," he muttered, as he turned onto the main road, farther from where we'd pulled off, making my tension warp into frustration at my inaction.

"I'm a princess. I can fix this," I said in my haughtiest, pre-tarnished voice.

His glance was enough for me to see the pity in his gaze.

I curled my lips in disgust. It was directed mostly at myself, but I was sick of feeling it. With him not wanting to get to know the real me mixed with his feeling bad for me, he was the perfect target. "Don't feel any distress on my behalf. Just because I'm different now, and no one in Envado likes it, doesn't mean I can't do anything."

"You're putting words in my mouth." His reaction was as heated as mine.

"Oh, am I? Then why do I see pity in your eyes?"

"You don't know me well enough to say what is there." His eyes flashed angrily.

Had I misread him?

Even if I had, I needed to gain control of the situation, so I could help the tarnished. That was what mattered, not my personal feelings. "Where are the other locations? I'm not asking again."

He sighed. "I'm beginning to wonder if I made a mistake, bringing you in on this."

I pursed my lips but gave him another moment to answer.

Mila didn't. "We can't sit by and do nothing. We need more information."

This time, when Lonvar looked at me, his expression was sorrowful. "I'm afraid no one will believe you, because of who is leading the trouble."

A pang of worry smacked into my chest. "Just tell me."

"The whole plot was instigated and is run at the command of Prince Rumam."

My brother, hurting tarnished for his own gain? The thought made bile rise in my throat. "How do you know?"

"I've heard it from the mouths of those close to the royal court. It's one of the reasons he travels so much."

As much as I didn't want to believe Lonvar and didn't know if I could fully trust him, it made a horrific sort of sense. And I would not put up with it.

CHAPTER 7

I plastered my court mask on. "Why bring me in on this?"

"I'm sorry."

I stared at him, wanting answers, not apologies.

"I needed you to believe me so you'd help me get closer to your brothers."

"You know I'm not close to them."

He turned the wheel as he rounded a bend in the road. "Perhaps not, but you're the closest link I have."

I didn't like it. I'd rather get close to them myself.

"Get me to the palace." It was probably where he was taking me anyway, but I wouldn't sit back and do nothing, while my brother—and probably both of them—took away the freedom of people who'd already been tortured.

Instead of listening, Lonvar pulled over to a side street and parked the motorcar at the side of a park, the type of green space I'd expected him to take me to instead of to see tarnished being brutalized.

He didn't get out of the motorcar.

"You have to take us to the castle," Mila said. "Now."

Instead, he turned toward me and said, "We can't confront your brother directly. Not without more evidence."

38

"What more evidence do you need? We all saw the tarnished being herded around." The words brought a flash of pain. I could have been one of those tarnished. I had been. "We've got to save them."

"I agree, which is why I brought you into this. But whom will they believe? You, me, and Mila, or your brother? And without proof?"

I cringed at the way he put it. The thought of not being believed made me sick. I was too much a tarnished for anyone to take my warnings as real. My country—my very own brother—was as bad as the madman who'd first turned people tarnished. Perhaps worse, because we'd been taught better our entire lives.

He had a point. Who would believe me?

Dad would, but to what end? He held little power despite being king. Mother humored him, but only with things that weren't matters of state. Mila's words wouldn't have much more impact than mine. She might be my guard, but she was also my lady's maid. My mother never took her near as seriously as she should, but I'd never thought it would matter. Never thought I'd be in a position such as this.

What we really needed was my mother involved, and I couldn't see her implicating her son without hard evidence against him. I rubbed the back of my neck. "Say I believe you, and that we need evidence. How are we supposed to get it?"

"I need you to get me close to Rumam."

I gave a cold laugh. "Wrong person to ask."

"But you're closer to him than you know. At least physically, you have access to him. The ball proved that your brother is interested in your life."

I frowned. "Only when I get more attention than they do."

"Maybe. Maybe not."

"What do you mean?"

"They could have come over to you because of that, or because they hadn't seen you since you left Envado. Maybe there's something else going on. Time will tell, but if you can insert yourself

39

into their lives and plans, perhaps we can get the information we need."

I glanced back at Mila.

She shrugged. "He might have a point."

Didn't mean I had to like it. People were suffering more with every moment it took me to get close to Rumam. "It'd be worth a try," I said. I couldn't believe I started the day thinking he was interested in me as a woman. That would have been a change.

He looked away, his grip tight on the steering wheel.

Not like it made a difference that he wasn't attracted to me. There were more important things to be done, and I didn't have time to waste pondering the feelings of a man I hardly knew. "It's time for you to take me home."

"But we haven't made a plan fo—"

"Take me home." I didn't want to hear it. I would deal with my brother without his help, no matter the toll it took on me. Even if I'd wanted his attention, I wasn't getting it, so no sense mooning over him. What would my friends back in Chardonia think if they could see me now?

Without another word, Lonvar started the motorcar and drove away, past buggies and people strolling. There had to be an answer, to put me in a position to help the tarnished. Both the ones my brother was taking and the ones who came to Envado looking for hope and a better life.

Until I found those answers, I'd have to struggle along, doing my best. Alone.

The guards let us through the castle gates, and Lonvar pulled up in front of the doors. Before he'd come to a stop, they opened, and my brothers bounded down the stairs, Rumam with a big grin on his face.

I jumped out of the car with a murmured "thank you" to Lonvar, dismissing him. Instead of going, he got out of the motorcar and met me and Mila around the side, where my brothers waited.

"This bloke again, sis? Didn't know you were serious about anyone," Rumam said.

Herni, who usually fell more into the background when a crowd was near, gave Lonvar a long stare.

I rolled my eyes. "You two are being silly. We just went to a nearby park and chatted."

"It's a pleasure to meet you again." Lonvar gave each of them a long bow.

This time, I held in the eye roll. I might not have known Lonvar well, but I understood him enough to know that a bow like that wasn't his style. Trying to get on my brothers' good sides, no doubt.

Ignoring him, I headed for the door. It'd be best if my brothers would follow.

They didn't.

"Who are you?" Rumam asked.

Lonvar said, "It's a pleasure to make the acquaintance of the brothers of such a beautiful woman. Your sister is like no one I've ever met before."

I tightened my hands into fists and turned back toward the conversation, ready to snap back with something moody. He was obviously trying to get on their good side, but he forgot one thing. They didn't like me.

Rumam beat me to a comeback with, "You have the wrong woman. This sister of mine has no beauty remaining, though it appears she still has the same spunk as when she left."

My hand flew before I realized what I was doing, and I smacked Rumam in the back of the head.

"*Ow.*" He shot me a glare. "What was that for? Nobody hits the crown prince."

"Sisters do, when he needs it, and you know very well what that was for. Don't be rude."

He rubbed where I'd hit, before telling Lonvar, "See? All spunk and bite. There's nothing soft there. Trust me, you don't want anything to do with her."

"Shut your mouth." I strode back to Lonvar's side and crossed my arms over my chest. "It's no use, trying to scare him off. If he didn't run when he saw your ugly face last night, nothing will frighten him."

"Take a look in the mirror, sister." Rumam's words came out lightly, but they struck their place regardless. Not that I would let him see it.

"I see you're just the same as when I left."

"And you're a little worse for the wear."

I was fuming and wanted to deck him. Mila looked as if she felt the same, though she'd stuck to the sidelines, like she was supposed to.

Lonvar took my fist in his hand.

When did I uncross my arms? Startled, I raised my gaze to him.

He kept his own locked on my eldest brother. "I'm certain the princess will understand if we decide to take things inside."

Oh no. I'd much rather show Rumam my fists out here. Then again, those walking by the castle could see through the gates. I didn't turn to look, but it was likely that at least a few onlookers were watching. I might not like my brother, but others did. Landing a good one wouldn't win me any favors. I'd lost enough of those. If I wanted any help with the tarnished, I probably shouldn't push my luck any further.

"Yes, dear brothers. Why don't we take this inside?" I gave them a wicked grin, promising my rage when we were somewhere more appropriate for it.

It wouldn't be the first time we fought, but it had been many years since we physically brawled.

"I'd rather talk more to Lonvar. Why don't you run along and do whatever it is tarnished do these days?" Rumam dismissed me easily enough, yet his eyes flashed the promise of a fight later.

Apparently, he was as aware of possible onlookers as I was. They weren't the ones who bothered me. I didn't want to squabble with Rumam when he was so hateful toward me. I had better things to do, and Lonvar had wanted time with my brothers. I'd give it to him while I took matters to the person who'd really make a difference.

The queen.

CHAPTER 8

Mila and I went on a furious search. We hustled through the castle, servants giving me sidelong glances. It might not be very princess-like of me, but then, neither was it royal-like to use tarnished in such a way as my brother supposedly did. Mother would know what to do if it was Rumam. If not, I'd find proof of him or whoever it was behind the plot and make certain they paid for what they were doing.

Mother wasn't in her chambers, the sitting room, the dining room, or the throne room. So much for that idea. I'd have to find her at the earliest possible moment. We couldn't let my brother go on like he was.

Too many thoughts ran through me. It was clear the tarnished were held against their will, and there had been talk of testing them. What was that about?

I should have spent more time grilling Lonvar.

I reached the business chambers, where my mother counseled with members of the court, and came to a stop before closed doors. There was a guard on either side.

I asked, "Is my mother in there?"

Neither answered me, but the fact that they were here sent a clear signal that she was inside. My news was important enough

44

for me to burst in. It was tempting, but she wouldn't appreciate it, even if it was the direst situation.

Arms at her sides, Mila stepped back against the opposite wall, far too quiet to let me know what was going on in her head.

I paced along the hall, under the guards' watchful gaze. I wanted to demand answers out of them, but I'd been foolish to ask in the first place. Guards rarely spoke when on duty protecting the queen. The walls pressed in on me, making me want to scream. I needed to talk to Mother an hour ago, when I first discovered the tarnished were being held captive.

The minutes ticked by, until finally the door opened, and a laughing, rotund man came out. "Thank you, Your Majesty. I will be in contact soon." His laughter stopped abruptly, as he saw me.

"Excuse me. I need to speak with my mother." I would have pushed the man, but that would only earn a lecture from her.

The man's gaze zeroed in on me. "Ah, yes. Please." He moved out of the way, motioning for me to go in.

I didn't spare him another glance, as I hurried in and Mila came in after me. She followed and closed the door behind her.

"To what do I owe this pleasure?" Mother didn't look up from her writing as I rushed toward where she sat at her desk.

Mila took a more respectful stance at the back of the room, where she'd still be able to hear everything. I knew because I'd been at that back wall many times in my life, while Mother discussed planning events, affairs of state, and laws with others.

I clutched the edge of her desk with both hands, leaning closer. "Tarnished are being gathered in the woods near here, though I suppose in other places around Envado too."

She still didn't look up from what she was writing, though she slowed. "Is that so?"

"Yes. Mila can vouch for everything I saw. It was terrible. I don't know what's happening to them, but there was hitting and people guarding them and—" The horror of everything I went through in Chardonia came smacking into me, almost knocking me over.

45

Mother lifted her head. "And?"

My mouth ran dry, and my head felt funny, like I might faint.

"And it's true." Mila came to my rescue. "It was an atrocity."

"I see." Mother frowned.

She didn't, though. If she did, she'd be far more upset. "You're not hearing what I'm saying."

Finally, she put her pen down and gave me her full attention. "By all means, please enlighten me about what you know."

My tongue felt dry. "Tarnished are being abducted. I saw them."

Mother folded her hands primly on the desk with a sigh. "Darling, this isn't Chardonia." Her voice might have been soft, but the words were a jagged cut to my heart. She continued. "I'm not barbaric, like their Grand Chancellor was. I know what's going on in my country, and I am dealing with it. Certain things cannot be handled overnight. It's a process."

"But the tarnished need help now," I insisted.

Her next sigh came out even heavier. "You've been through a lot—more than your father or I will ever understand. What those horrid Chardonians did to you... Well, it shouldn't have happened. But for you to project your fears onto things I'm taking care of isn't healthy. Have you spoken to anyone else about this?"

Lonvar's name hovered on the edge of my tongue, but I couldn't bring myself to drag him into this and let him know how right he was that I shouldn't have said anything. "I have not. Does this mean you know who's the mastermind of the plot, too?" She had to know at least one of her sons was behind it, if she knew all this, but I had to ask.

She gave me a somewhat indulgent, patient smile. "Yes, Tawny."

She stood and stepped around the desk to face me and put her hands on my shoulders. "It would be best if you talked to someone who... understands what you went through."

"Like other tarnished? I've thought about speaking with the

refugees. They could use someone in a position like mine, to listen to them."

"Yes, dear. Why don't you do that? In the meantime, if you need any help, you come to me."

Tension seeped out of me. There were things I could still do. Ways I could help, without getting in her way or disrupting her handling of the situation. In the meantime, I could warn other refugees.

Mother linked arms with me, patted my hand, and headed toward the door. She said, "You're dismissed for now, Mila. Thank you for taking care of my daughter."

"Of course." Mila bowed and left.

Once we were out in the hall, headed back toward the royal wing with her guards following close behind, Mother said, "We'll find a place for you here in the palace where you can be of assistance to me, Tawny. You're the princess..." Silence stretched out uncomfortably, making me think she had more to say.

When she said nothing, I tried to encourage her with, "That's true."

She sighed, as if heavily burdened. "Have you thought of putting makeup over your tattoos? I set some out for you, but... And we should also have the royal physician look over your baldness. I'm certain a woman of her caliber could get your hair to grow again."

My cheeks flushed. I wanted to rage against this; why couldn't my mother just accept who I was? But my mother always got her way, no matter how hard I tried. This had only gotten worse over the years, yet it was because she loved me and wanted the best for me. Oh, she let me get away with certain outfits or outings, but only if she wasn't truly against them.

That was what now had me saying, "If it would make you feel better, I would be willing."

"It would make us both feel better. You'll be much more yourself, once we cover up this condition of yours."

I gulped down the fears clawing their way up my throat. They

47

scratched, leaving raw emotions on the way back down. Nothing could cover up what I was. It was as much a part of me as the need to breathe. But if the queen wished for it to be hidden, I didn't have a choice. So I could only nod in response.

We turned down a hall, to find my brothers walking toward us. Lonvar was between them, with a stupid grin on his face.

"Mother, dearest." Rumam bent over and kissed the back of her hand. "What is our sister going on about now?"

Mother waved her hand dismissively. "You know your sister, always up to something."

I gritted my teeth.

"We have good plans for her, going forward." She patted my hand.

She only wanted what was best for me, but these plans weren't it. "Where's Dad?" I asked.

"He's gone off to his hunting lodge," Mother said.

Without saying goodbye? "Oh."

"He'll be back in his own time. Now be a dear and run along with your brothers. I have matters to attend."

She slipped away from me, toward her rooms. The loneliness left me feeling more lost than ever.

CHAPTER 9

I was stuck with these warlocks again.

Rumam and Herni spoke quietly to each other, Lonvar pitching in a sentence now and again. Mostly, though, Lonvar watched me warily, but I didn't want to deal with him. He'd gotten in with my brothers, more than I was in any case, and obviously had what he wanted.

I needed some space, to figure this all out. I sighed and headed toward my rooms.

"Where are you going, sis?" Herni called out.

"Away." I heard something that sounded like *spoilsport*. Ignoring my brothers' attempt to barb me, I hurried down the hall. My frustration mounted once I was behind a closed door, but there was nowhere I could release the tension, despite being in my own rooms.

Forcing myself to walk calmly, I went to my bed, crawled onto it, buried my face into the pillow, and screamed. The tarnished needed help. Mother was doing something, but I wanted to be involved, and she wasn't going to hear of it.

I stayed in my room the rest of the night, claiming I didn't feel well. And I didn't. I might not have been ill, but I was heartsick. I and so many, *many* others had been put in my terrible situation.

49

We couldn't even have children, because of what the depravers had done to us with their magic.

We were marked on the outside and torn up on the inside, figuratively and literally. The shivers running through me shook my bed. I shut my eyes tight, willing awful memories to go away. It took hours of trying to stop reliving the horrors I'd gone through. That others had dealt with as well.

I got up early in the morning, done wallowing. My self-pity wouldn't help the tarnished.

The first thing I needed to do was hunt down that blasted Lonvar. Yes, he told me the truth about the tarnished, but only because I was a tarnished, and as a way to get at my brothers. He didn't even try to stop me when I stormed off yesterday.

To think I'd even been attracted to him. Ugh.

Throwing on a pair of breeches and a blouse, I went to grab a brush, only to remember I didn't have hair anymore. My hands shook as I ran them down my thighs to straighten my clothes. It'd been a long time since I'd forgotten about my baldness for even a moment. Being at home must have reverted me to who I once was, hair and all.

I grabbed the brush off my dresser, opened the window, and hucked the brush outside.

That felt better. Why was there a brush in my room, anyway?

With long strides, I hurried out of the castle, ignoring the onlookers. There were more than just servants about, this morning, since there hadn't been a ball last night leaving revelers exhausted.

Now that I was outside, I realized I hadn't a clue where to go or what to do. Lonvar had to be somewhere in the city, but I hadn't the faintest idea where. I shouldn't have abandoned him so readily when he had far more answers than I did.

It took a moment's indecision, before I decided to barge in on my brothers. One—I'd last seen Lonvar with them, and since he wanted to be close to my brothers, it seemed likely they would know something. Two—I also wanted to get close to them and find out if they were really involved. Three—it would annoy them this early in the morning, and that was reason enough for me to do so.

I made my way to the royal wing. Should I go to Herni's suite or Rumam's? The latter seemed more involved in things, and Herni followed him everywhere, so I chose Rumam's door to pound on.

After counting to twenty with no answer, I burst in, grateful the door gave in so easily.

"What?" Herni mumbled from the couch in Rumam's sitting room.

"Rise and shine, big brother. It's a beautiful day."

There was a groan from the couch facing away from me. Rumam. Had they been drinking or just staying up late? Either way, they were ridiculous for not making it to their beds before settling in for the night, but it'd make my job easier, so I wouldn't complain.

I walked over to the back of the couch, bent down toward the person there, and was mulling over what was wrong with the situation when Lonvar's eyes popped open, inches from mine.

With a squeak, I jumped. "What are you doing in here?"

"What are you doing, waking people up by getting in their face?" he grumbled back.

Not about to answer that, I straightened my blouse that didn't need straightening and said, "I didn't know you were in here."

"Spent time with your brothers until so late last night, the Crown Prince said I could borrow his couch if I wanted."

"You should have gone home." Secretly, I was grateful I wouldn't have to track him down.

"Can you two shut up?" Herni groaned.

"Oh, the sun's almost crested the horizon. Surely, we can be up now," I said, plopping onto the couch next to his feet.

With another groan, he kicked me, though not hard enough to hurt.

51

"We went to bed late," Lonvar said. "Or rather, early this morning."

That wasn't a surprise, but it did leave me wondering how Lonvar wormed his way into my brothers' good graces—and how I could do the same.

"We should go on a picnic," I said.

Herni squinted at me. "It's too blasted early."

"For lunch, then. I'll pack us a basket. Lonvar can trail along if you like." Might as well get close to my brothers *and* Lonvar while I could manage it. I'd still have to find time to speak with Lonvar privately. I'd ignore the pull I felt toward him and get more answers.

"Only if it will get you to let us sleep more," Herni said.

I took in my brother—clothes wrinkled from sleep, lanky form twisted up on the couch, and boots on the floor beside him. What was his part in the tarnished kidnappings? "I'll give you till one, but if all three of you aren't in the courtyard then, I'll be pounding on the door to get you." I bounced to my feet. "Make sure Rumam knows."

Herni gave a relieved sigh as I hurried to the hall without another word from either him or Lonvar.

There had to be a way I could pump my brothers for information, if they really were involved. For all I knew, Lonvar had made that up. Except, why would he?

I spent my morning plotting, until the time to meet grew near. After fetching enough food for the four of us from the cook, I headed outside and had a four-person motorcar brought around. It was a sleek, shiny black model, with a fold-down top which left the passengers open to the air. I liked it.

When the clock struck one, I was ready.

My brothers and Lonvar must have taken my threat to heart because three minutes later, they meandered out.

Herni gave me a sleepy nod.

Lonvar's gaze stayed on me but his expression remained neutral.

Rumam surprised me. He gave one of his too bright smiles the girls hung on and strode straight to me. "Good morning, sis."

I snorted. "More like *afternoon*."

He shrugged. "Either way. Shall we?" He motioned toward the motorcar.

Before anyone could protest, I jumped in the driver's seat.

"Oh no," Herni said. "I'm not going if you're driving."

Sure, it'd been some time, but one didn't forget how to. "It'll be fantastic," I said.

"Don't forget, I was there when you learned to drive," he replied.

"Was she awful?" Lonvar asked, climbing in the motorcar behind me, while Rumam took the seat next to me.

I scoffed. "I was never awful."

"More like wildly reckless." Herni stared at the three of us.

"Come or not. I'm going." With a flick of my wrist, I started the engine.

With a curse, Herni got in the back. Before he'd finished closing the door, we were off.

The windshield protected the front of the car, but air still whipped past me from the side and exposed top.

I laughed as I pulled out of the castle drive and onto the street. I was careful of the people, horses, and other vehicles on the street, yet Herni's continued grumblings would have made anyone think I was entirely reckless.

Businesses and then houses seemed to fly by. Excitement pumped through me. I might have had three men I didn't know as well as I needed to with me—two of whom were my brothers who might be doing nefarious things—but for the moment, I didn't care. I let the thrumming beneath me fill me with energy to go fast.

When the road cleared, I pressed down on the pedal and shifted into a higher gear.

Herni gulped.

"Really, you'd think I was mad." I laughed, probably not helping my case. "If anyone is a crazy driver, it's Rumam."

He flashed those shiny teeth at me again. "Only you, dear sister, would dare say such a thing."

"I know how to treat a dear brother." I widened my grin until I probably looked deranged and focused my gaze—but not my mind—back on the road. Rumam wasn't just a spoiled, bratty, annoying older brother, but also a fiend who was dangerous to others according to Lonvar. I wished to show my true feelings toward him, to demand answers for all the tarnished who were being put through even more after they'd already gone through so much. Yet I had to keep myself put together until I had more answers.

Where to take them? As the wind swept through my hair and the greenery blurred by, it was difficult to decide.

I didn't want to take them to the spot where Lonvar took me yesterday. That'd be foolhardy if my brothers were truly involved. Besides, I wasn't certain I could get back there without Lonvar's help. I practically grew up in these mountains, when I wasn't in the castle, so I had more ideas.

Opting for the view I'd wanted to see since I left Envado, even though I'd rather not share it with these three, I made a turn and headed up a different side canyon than where Lonvar took us yesterday.

It'd be a beautiful day, no matter what came. I'd make it that way.

We bounced over the road for several miles, while the land rose around us. The canyon stretched wide across the ground but left plenty of room for us to drive next to the river. The rush of the waterfall grew close enough we could hear it over the puttering of the car.

Moments later, we arrived.

Herni scrambled out of the car first, swaying on his feet.

"It wasn't that bad," I said.

He looked at me, a pale-green tint to his face. Maybe I had been a little crazy, but then, no one else seemed to think so.

Except, the other men weren't getting out yet.

I shrugged, hopped out, made my way over to the pool by the falls, and sighed. This was what I wanted. Needed. Peace and serenity. A place to recharge.

The peacefulness of it soothed me, even as a cool breeze brushed against my scalp, reminding me of what I was now. There was always a reminder. And with Mother's suggestion at my lack of grace at the ball, perhaps I did need to change things.

A branch snapped, and then hands shoved me from behind. I teetered on the edge of the bank, before plunging down into the water.

CHAPTER 10

I sputtered, icy water licking my skin. I scrambled out onto dry land as Rumam laughed hysterically. Shivering, I glared at him. "I didn't bring a change of clothes."

"I couldn't resist. Besides, it might be cold mountain water, but it's a warm day." He continued chuckling.

"Just remember—turnabout's fair play."

Lonvar was at my side. In low tones he asked, "Are you all right?"

"Fine." The word shot out of me, but I didn't care. So much for enjoying myself.

I worked on wringing water out of my blouse, while the men gathered and spoke. I should be glad I didn't have long locks to wring out as well, but mostly, I felt cold and ornery.

I slipped away. I followed a slim path and ducked behind the waterfall it led to. I was already wet, so getting a little more so wouldn't make a difference. The little cave was just tall enough for my height, and I almost brushed my head against it. I wrapped my arms around myself to keep warm and watched the water splashing down.

Coming here with them wasn't going to get me on my brothers' good sides. I was too much of me and they were too much of them. Stupid Rumam, pushing me in. Bringing them here had been a mistake. I should have attempted to find where the tarnished were taken, and faced the guards there with hard questions.

Lonvar entered the space, ducking his head. "It's nice back here."

I snorted. "Other than not being able to stand. Why don't you go back to my brothers?"

"Because you and I need to talk."

I gave him a flat look.

"Look," he said, barely audible above the roar of the waterfall. "You were the one who left me with them. Remember?" His heated gaze did funny things to my stomach.

"And you took the chance and ran. You don't need me anymore. You should be out there, cozying up to the Grand Chancellor lovers, not bickering with me," I said.

"Just because they're abusing the tarnished from Chardonia doesn't mean they love the Grand Chancellor."

I pursed my lips. "And yet, that doesn't stop them from doing horrible things. I mean, what type of person kidnaps others and abuses them? Do you know why he's doing it?"

"Not yet, but we'll find out." He held my gaze.

The *we* warmed me. "What's their purpose in taking tarnished?"

He rubbed his eyes. "I haven't been able to figure that out. The kidnappers seem to bring in tarnished and then they disappear."

"Disappear or are they..." Killed. I didn't want to say it though.

"If they wanted them dead and nothing else, they could do that when they took them. No reason to bring them all together and keep them around. No, there's something else going on."

"Is there another place in the forest we could go to learn more?" I shivered from the cold.

"I'm not taking you around another encampment. It's too risky. The best thing you can do is get information from your brothers."

I waved him away. "They're more likely to give you information than me."

"All I've gotten so far is that they are frivolous. Well, Herni is more serious, but is livening up the longer I'm around."

"Sounds like them. But you've gotten closer to them in a day than I ever was. I've only ever watched them from the outside. You got what you needed from me, so you may as well return to spying on them."

The look he gave me was difficult to understand. It was almost like longing. But we didn't even know each other. He really did want to use me, though I didn't yet know how.

I faced forward, staring at the waterfall.

"If you're sure, I'll go, but there's a lot more you can do than you think."

"I want to help. I will, so don't exclude me. I simply think you'll be able to get closer to my brothers than I will, and you said yourself that was why you showed them to me."

Out of the corner of my eye, I saw him watching me. My muscles were stiff, my mind focused on keeping my gaze straight ahead at the water. I jolted in surprise when he took a hold of my shoulder, his skin warm through the material.

"There are things I should say to you, but for now, know that I do enjoy spending time with you." A second later, he added, "Even if you're like a race car driver, in your need for speed."

His hand continued to warm me, making me wish I knew him well enough to embrace him. To feel more of his body heat. Instead, I stood there stoically.

With one great sigh, he slipped back toward the others, away from the curtain of water.

I dropped my shoulders. He was right. I did need to get to know my brothers better. To join their circle. But Rumam's shoving me in the water was proof they didn't want me here, despite my being the one who brought them. Unless he thought it was just a joke.

Didn't matter. I would learn to deal with them if it meant

saving others like me. I straightened my back and went out from behind the waterfall. Once I was on the bank, the sun warmed my skin, chasing away my goose bumps. I hadn't realized just how cold I'd gotten.

The men had stripped down to their trousers and were taking turns jumping in, like they were still boys instead of almost adults. Legally, that happened when they turned nineteen, but they didn't act like it. My brothers were easy enough to ignore, but my gaze was drawn to Lonvar. I purposefully avoided looking at him, not wanting my attraction to him to grow any stronger than it already had.

I hesitated on the edge of joining them. I was already wet, but my stomach grumbled. So I headed to the motorcar, to fetch the picnic basket. It would be good to observe them.

I found a flat rock, spread a blanket out beside it, in case the others wanted it, and popped open the basket. The rock was the perfect size. I made myself comfortable on it and crunched into an apple, the sweetness tickling my tongue. The air smelled fresh, without a hint of a breeze. My clothes were drying.

The men splashed about happily, dunking each other and jumping in with the biggest splash yet. I watched for a while, but it continued on as more of the same for a good hour before Rumam got out, shook off, and came over to plop on the blanket next to me.

"You're still wet, you'll soak the blanket." How else should I respond to his presence? I wanted to fight him, rage against him, or shove *him* in the water. It'd get me nowhere.

He waved a hand and reached for a meat pie. "It'll dry." Expression growing more thoughtful, he turned toward me. "I shouldn't have pushed you in."

I whipped my head toward him, certain I looked startled but not caring enough to hide it. "Was that an apology?"

He shrugged, took a huge bite, and talked with his mouth full, like he wasn't the future king of Envado. "If you'd like."

I shook my head. "You're useless."

He clenched his jaw. "At least *I* didn't go gallivanting off to another country that was experiencing political turmoil."

"At least I did something about it."

"And look where that got you." I expected him to sneer, but his gaze was downcast.

I wouldn't let his sorrow affect me. "I helped *hundreds* of tarnished escape from a cruel living or found a place for them when the Grand Chancellor died—sometimes both—while your pretty face stayed here and attended balls." Heat rolled off me in waves as I huffed at him, my entire body rigid.

He had the presence of mind to feign a sheepish expression. He couldn't truly feel bad for what he'd done, but he couldn't very well say that, either.

He set down the half-eaten pie and rubbed his face. "I am sorry."

His tone was so sincere, it caught me off guard. "For what?"

"For everything. For not seeing the troubles going on around me. For not stepping up and going to help in your stead. For not protecting you from becoming..."

"Tarnished?" The word came out softer than I intended. Maybe this was my chance to get through to him, though for the life of me, why was he apologizing now? "You can say it. We're people, just like you, no matter what was taught in Chardonia."

He stared at Lonvar and Herni, who were getting out of the water and wringing themselves off. As the two headed our way, Rumam gave a soft, "I'm beginning to see that."

It was hard to hear that, knowing it meant he'd believed the worst about us just because we were visibly bald and inked, but his words also softened my heart. Maybe there was hope for the tarnished, if even he could admit to that.

Herni said, "Where's the food? I'm famished."

Lonvar gave me a long look. I gave him a slight nod when my brothers turned their attention to the basket. We would find a way to make Rumam understand how wrong what they were doing was. And we would save the tarnished.

CHAPTER 11

Rumam drove us back to the city, much to Herni's relief. I was content to sit in the back, beside Lonvar, and think about what Rumam had said. It was a side of him I'd never seen. Nothing like it had ever manifested in him before. If he truly did feel remorse, there was more hope then I'd believed.

We stopped to drop Lonvar off at his house, while I made a mental note of where it was. The home was a quaint little thing, connected to another house on each side. The brick exterior showed two floors, the lower one with a large window and the upper with three small ones. Though narrow, Lonvar's section of the house looked well maintained and orderly from the outside.

We drove back to the castle, and my brothers were immediately ushered inside to change, as they had a meeting to deal with. No one paid me any mind.

Which was fine. Totally fine.

I spent the next several days feeling a jumble of good and frustrated. Every time the three of us would spend time with Lonvar and Mila in the background, my brothers didn't seem to care that I inserted myself into their free moments. They were good times, my brothers warming up to me as much as I was to them.

After we stayed out as long as they dared, we'd rush off home so my brothers could help with important matters the queen arranged for them. I used to assist some too, but Mother thought I needed time to readjust.

Getting to know my brothers and Lonvar better was more fun than I expected. They all seemed like good men, stopping to help change a flat tire for a stranded group, giving coins to children, and being kinder than I'd expected. Lonvar made sense, but my brothers, why had I never noticed their kindness before? It made it hard for me to believe that Rumam and possibly Herni were involved in something nefarious. But if they weren't, it would mean Lonvar was lying or misinformed, which from the little I knew of him seemed just as improbable. Then again, he appeared to be completely at ease with them, so perhaps he was a good liar.

Something wasn't adding up, but I couldn't tell what. Or perhaps it was my own wishful thinking.

Lonvar... He was another puzzle all his own. The way my heart sped up around him, it was easy to tell the attraction I felt was growing. He picked me wildflowers in the area we hiked through yesterday. I'd never been given wild ones before. Sure, men sent me lots of store-bought flowers over the years, but the fact that he took the time to pick them himself left me giddy and lighthearted. Yet there wasn't time to have a crush on him when I was still working on winning my brothers over and assisting the tarnished.

I was pondering that one afternoon, after we returned from another hike in the mountains—Herni's idea—when there was a knock on my sitting-room door.

Mila answered with a curtsy.

A spark of hope lit in me at the possibility of seeing my dad. I had dinner with him last night, when he got back from the hunting lodge, but both my parents had responsibilities just as my brothers did. Everyone seemed to keep busy, except me.

I missed my old position of aiding my mother with responsibilities, but every time I tried to help, she turned me down. Though I understood that she wanted me to have time to recover, sitting around doing nothing left me agitated.

Before I finished hurrying over my mother stepped in the room. With a flick of her wrist, she dismissed Mila, who hurried off. Mila was certain to return soon, to help me ready for another ball tonight—this one, in honor of a courtier I didn't know. I would still be expected to attend with good graces.

"Afternoon, Mother," I said, as she took the most uncomfortable chair in the room—the one I previously used to make suitors I didn't like sit in. There hadn't been any of those since I returned. Except perhaps Lonvar, who I'd never tell to use that chair.

"No time for niceties, Tawny. Sit down." Her stern tone made me wonder what horrible thing was in store. I had a bad feeling it had to do with tonight's ball and our talk about the last one. Once I was settled, she continued. "I'm having items for the ball brought in. You will use them and wear them."

I clenched my teeth, so I didn't say something I shouldn't. We'd had this conversation before, but she apparently still remembered my initial reaction, easily changing my mind to something she wouldn't appreciate.

"I know it's hard for you, but it's also for the best."

"Perhaps, but maybe if the court got used to seeing me as a tarnished, it wouldn't be so bad."

She stiffened—the only hint she didn't agree. "You've already been gallivanting where people can see you, and the gossips love putting you down. Putting the whole family down."

No wonder she was upset. Appearances were what she lived for, but if I could get her to see my point of view, she might change her mind. "But Mother, I—"

"If you choose to disobey me again, Mila will be dismissed and replaced."

Careful not to show my feelings, I raged on the inside. Mila was fun-loving and caring. She shouldn't lose her job because I didn't want to wear makeup. And a wig—*ugh*. "I understand, but with your permission, I would like to wear a dress of my own choosing. I always did in the past. That wouldn't be too much of a shock for people." Even if my bare face was.

She sniffed. "Very well, but for magic's sake, take time to put some spells on it."

Exactly what I was hoping to avoid, but I'd figure out something palatable. "Yes, Mother."

"Good. And I don't want you leaving early again. The crown needs to protect its name, and you're a part of that."

If this was how to go about that, I wasn't certain I wanted to play a part. Except it would help the tarnished if I managed to show the people I stood up to the expectations. I dropped my gaze to my lap, my fingers twined together on it. Was I play acting because I was supposed to or because I was starting to believe in the frivolities I used to? I didn't want to forget the people of Chardonia and all they'd gone through.

All I'd gone through.

And yet, I was a princess. Mother was right; I did have a place here in court, and there were certain expectations. Even if I didn't like that.

"I only do this because I love you," Mother said, voice tight with emotion.

I jerked my head up to look at her. A sheen of tears graced her eyes, something I'd never seen before. We weren't a family that often expressed love and caring, other than how my dad would bend over backwards to make certain everyone was happy. I could have done with him by my side through this conversation, but the pull between my mother and me would have been hard on him.

Mother cleared her throat. "Yes, well... La dee da. I have a country to run. I will see you tonight, suitably made up for the occasion."

I stood as she did. "Certainly. But may I first ask how things are coming along with the kidnapped tarnished? Any news?"

"None that I can share, but I'm doing what's needed. Your focus should be on how you can make a difference to the country."

"Yes, Mother." I lowered my head.

Expecting her to go straight for the door, I stayed where I was.

Mother headed for me and patted my shoulder. As awkward as it was, it offered a certain comfort. Without another word, she left the room.

Mila entered shortly thereafter. "Shall we get you ready?" she asked, a bit of fear in her eyes. She no doubt got the same warning I did.

I gave her a soft smile. "I look forward to it." The lie didn't sit well, but neither would the truth.

We spent the next few hours primping, priming, and painting. The dress I chose—another of Katherine's—was a soft blue that matched my eyes. The skirt was fuller than my last one, but still not as voluminous as those other ladies of the court would wear.

My best friends from childhood weren't even here, to support me while knowing my situation. I missed Waverly and Zade, the two Envadi who understood me, something fierce. At one time, I believed Zade and I would end up as family by marriage, but that was in the past. They both stayed in Chardonia to fix the place up, after the rampage of the mad Grand Chancellor. The man who'd ruled the country had been taken down seven months ago, but Chardonia was still healing, while my homeland was full of fancy people, driving their fancy motorcars and doing fancy things. It was disgusting.

And I was playing right into it.

"What spells would you like on it?" Mila asked while my back was toward the mirror. I didn't want to see myself yet, with all the paint she'd applied over my tattooed face.

"I'll manage them myself. Thank you."

She bit her lower lip but didn't protest. "Your wig, then?"

I gulped past the rock lodged in my throat. Why did it have to be so important that I do all this? I knew the answer but didn't understand it. Not like I used to. As with my mother, appearances were everything in court. Those who looked better, who showed their magic prowess, belonged to the ruling class. I no longer felt like I belonged there. Maybe I never had, and that was why I'd gone to Chardonia.

I wanted to go for a fast drive, but I sat serenely—as I should—and said, "Yes. My wig, please."

Her eyes were sad as she returned, reached behind me, and retrieved the wig. She slipped it over my head and adjusted it over the smoothness of my scalp. It felt awkward and itchy. I drummed my fingers across my lap, to keep from using them to take it off.

"Anything else I can help you with, Princess?" Mila asked.

I shook my head, long black hair like my mother's flowing around my shoulders in carefully curled waves that went down to my elbows. Leaving hair down wasn't the fashion for balls nowadays, but Mother probably wanted to show off my fake locks and make me seem more *normal*. Didn't she realize there was a new *normal* in my life?

Mila curtsied. "I'll be a spell away, if you need me," she said and went out the servants' entrance.

I didn't want to look at myself like this, and yet, I couldn't help but turn slowly on the stool I sat upon. The mirror crept into my vision, until I dared look at myself.

Only it wasn't me. Not the current me.

Sitting tall and regal, I appeared almost like my old self. My eyes looked big—they always did—but somehow weren't my own, as they stared back at me with something akin to fear. The hair was darker than my usual shade, catching a blue sheen in the light from the ebbing rays of sun. Still, the way it curled around my face and slipped down in ringlets befitted my position.

And yet, if you looked closer, it was apparent something was off. The black tattoos tried to burn through the makeup like acid. They were faintly visible as if even the multiple layers of makeup weren't enough to hide my shame. Shame which I'd brought upon myself, in going to Chardonia when I was warned not to.

I shuddered and looked away. Despite wanting to be done, I had to cast at least a couple flashy spells, to keep Mother happy. Starting with casting one on my fingers, I flashed out a spell that was an angrier red than I expected. It encircled several of my fingers, making the skin glow and shine like there were jewels there, but really it was just magic, enhancing my skin.

I did the same for a necklace and stood without bothering to look in the mirror. Those spells didn't need much attention to get right. I'd done them perfectly many times over, before I left home. Casting them couldn't be that different from before.

I added sparkling, color-changing nails and a shimmer to the skin of my arms and neck. With a sharp eye, I examined the details of my dress. It already had a glow to it, and the detail work on the bodice was exquisite. Taking care to calm as much of my anger as I could, I let the last spell fly. It was mostly yellow this time, with only hints of red. I didn't want to think much on what the new color meant, but it popped into my thoughts anyway. *Coward.*

I was giving in instead of standing up, but I had to, for Mila's sake and for my mother's.

The spell responded as I'd wanted, my knowledge of how to cast it long ingrained in my mind—since I was a little child and first started spelling my dresses. Of course, doing one's own spells ran out of fashion at some point, giving way to servants doing them for the upper class, so the latter could save their powers for whatever event they were to attend.

I snorted and watched the detail work on the bodice, the patterned swirls coming to life with a flash of brilliance that dimmed before more flashed into existence. It still wasn't much, but it should be enough to appease Mother. If not, I would hear about it in the family's waiting chamber.

I slipped on the silver shoes Mila left for me and headed toward that room. I was earlier this time, as I didn't want to get her in any more trouble by being late.

Mother and Dad were waiting, but my brothers were nowhere to be seen.

As the door closed behind me, Mother cast a critical, queenly eye over me. She frowned at my dress, and her frown only deepened when she got to my face. She wanted the makeup to cover more than it did, no doubt, but it should be good enough for the dimmer lights of the ball.

Dad, who had his back toward me, turned and jumped.

If I hadn't been so upset, I might have laughed.

"Tawny?" His tone was almost excited, but something held it back.

I forced a smile. "Mother had some things brought in for me."

Comprehension dawned on his face. "I see."

The room grew uncomfortably quiet, until a couple minutes later, Rumam and Herni burst in.

Rumam came over to me and said, "Darling sister, your dress is stunning. You will be the talk of the ball."

Was he serious? I'd be the talk all right, but not in a good way. And *stunning*? I must have wormed my way into his life more than I thought possible.

Herni gave me a nod.

"Now that you boys are here, we can finally go in." Mother took Dad's arm and led him toward the ballroom, where they were announced.

When my name was called out, I stepped forward after my brothers, feeling the thick paint on my face and the heaviness of my wig intensely. It felt as if the guests' gazes slipped past my family, slid to me, and stuck there.

The fake hair and layers of pigment grew even thicker and heavier. I kept a smile plastered on my face, but it felt as fake as the rest of me. People spoke to each other behind hands. Titters sounded throughout the hall.

Somehow, it was worse than when I'd come out fully as a tarnished. I wanted to scream and rage at my mother for forcing me to endure this, at myself for giving in, but I kept my cool.

Walked to my throne and took a seat on it, as if I belonged, when we all knew it was the furthest thing from the truth.

Blasted as I sat here being phony, while someone, possibly led by my brothers, was taking advantage of the tarnished. I felt more out of place than ever and didn't know what to do about it.

When my gaze landed on a tarnished, and then several more scattered throughout the crowd, my falseness felt heavier than ever. They'd never attended before. As much as I wanted them here, their stares at my fake appearance were heavier than the weight of the country.

I kept an eye out for them as the ball started with my brothers' going out to dance, except it was different than before. Or maybe not. Maybe I hadn't paid enough attention previously.

Herni's steps were hesitant, as he approached a potential dance partner. I was beginning to believe he was shy with how slowly he'd warmed up to me and his usual silence around others.

Rumam was the complete opposite, bounding to the most spelled lady in the hall and commandeering her to the floor. The shiny, thick locks of the woman were familiar—they belonged to the woman he danced with on the night of my homecoming ball. She looked demurely at him through her eyelashes, before sending a spell around them that flashed through the air with colors, drawing more attention. She should have been a good fit for him, but something about her made my blood run cold. I hoped he was more selective with whom he took for a bride to become the queen of Envado.

If I found the proof I needed to connect him to the tarnished kidnappings, he would never be king. My heart gave a little twist. I was beginning to like my brother, a little.

I was so intent on my thoughts and watching him, I didn't notice Lonvar until he was practically upon us. He bowed low to my mother and then my dad. "Your Majesties, it has been a pleasure, spending time with your family this week. The princes and princess have done me a great service, helping me learn more about our people as we enjoyed the sights around Envado."

The queen pursed her lips. "And you are?"

"Lonvar Dastik, Your Majesty."

"So you're the one that's been spending time with my children," Mother said, definitely still in queen mode. "You've had them gallivanting off early and staying out long enough the boys have missed some of their meetings."

"I'm afraid I have. I'll be more aware of the time in the future."

"And why is it you come to us now?" she asked. It was common for guests to talk with her at the ball, and he thanked them, so it was an odd question—if I didn't know her better. She had probably seen the same hesitance in him that I did about wanting something more.

His arms hung loosely at his sides, but if I wasn't mistaken, he was shaking slightly, despite the relaxed posture. He didn't seem nervous around anyone before, but it was different when you met the queen and king. I was so accustomed to it, the reminder surprised me.

He straightened his taut back further. "I would like to ask for the favor of being your daughter's first dance of the evening, if she would like it."

An honor usually given to my dad or some lucky soul who was high up in court—and none of the latter had come to ask for it yet, and it was well into the ball. It wasn't surprising, given my awkward state that everyone knew about but nobody could speak of.

"Hmm." The queen sounded disappointed to have such a small catch for my first dance.

"Let the boy dance with her," Dad said. He whispered something into Mother's ear.

With a gracious nod, she said, "Very well. Treat her like the jewel she is."

Despite the itching under my wig she made me wear, tenderness for her filled me.

"I promise, Your Majesties." And Lonvar turned his wonderfully brown eyes my way.

My heartbeat sped up, as our gazes met. Something sparked between us, almost like a current of electricity.

Lonvar, the man who only wanted to use to me to get close to my brothers...

And I was falling for him.

CHAPTER 12

I wanted to protest, as he asked me for my hand, but since the queen had already given her permission, it would have been a great shame to him. Besides, no one else was likely to ask, and he was my only link to finding out more about the tarnished.

But I wished I could say *no*. I didn't want to grow any fonder of him and his heart-melting smile.

Instead, I placed my hand in his, and together we found a spot on the dance floor. A splash of color filled the air and made the music echo through my body. I moved as I was supposed to. Lonvar was an even better dancer than I remembered. I wish I hadn't noticed.

I averted my gaze, only to find those still gathered around the room, waiting their turn to join the dance or sitting it out, watched us with eyes that missed nothing. Their sharp gazes pierced into me, the eyes watching with accusations I didn't want to understand. It was a wonder I didn't rip off my wig that very moment, throw it to the floor and stomp on it before marching away. Being this close to Lonvar and knowing he didn't feel the same as I did was torturous enough without all the judgmental courtiers.

Even Rumam's dance partner, with her beauty and spells, wasn't pulling the attention away from me. From over Rumam's shoulder, she sent a glare my way that wasn't softened by her bloodthirsty grin.

I jerked my focus back to Lonvar, and he locked his gaze on mine. It was the worst thing I could have done, as my heart thumped more loudly. The busybodies were a nuisance and could hurt me with their words even if I hadn't heard any tonight, and the glaring woman could lash out against me, but I had a feeling he could hurt me much worse.

"Do the tarnished usually attend balls? I believe this is the first time I've seen them," he asked.

I shook my head. "Someone must have invited them for my benefit. Dad, probably." Though it was a kind gesture, it left my heart aching that I hadn't done more for them. That I was hiding the fact I was the same as them.

"I'm glad you consented to dancing with me," he said as we slid across the floor that was magicked to show our footprints for a good ten seconds, before they slowly faded. I'd always thought it made for a romantic sight, but now I wished the fad had died away while I was gone.

"You doubted I would?" I asked lightly.

He lifted his eyebrows the slightest bit, before he relaxed again. "After all the time we spent together the past week? I hoped you would say yes." He pulled me slightly closer, and my stomach gave a flutter.

I didn't know whether to close the rest of the distance, so I could lay my head on his shoulder, or stiffly move away from him. In the end, I stayed where I was, except when he twirled me. The song was crescendoing. The music's end would come soon.

"We need to do something. My brothers are giving nothing away," I said.

Whatever was in his expression shuttered. "Getting them to open up has been harder than I thought."

73

"They were never so friendly, when we were growing up." I kept my voice low. Their actions could easily be faked now, but I wasn't certain that was the case. "There must be something we're not seeing with them and more going on with the tarnished we need to look for. I've been trying to puzzle it out, but haven't gotten anywhere."

A muscle ticked in his jaw, and I had the strong urge to run my finger across it. I focused on keeping my hand in his, enjoying the feel of his skin against mine. His hand was rough, calloused with work.

"What is your job?" I asked.

He averted his gaze. "Members of court don't do any real work."

I narrowed my eyes. "And are you a member of court? I hadn't seen you before, but I have been gone some time."

"I belong right where I am." This time, he did look back at me, a fire in his eyes that had me inching closer even as we danced across the floor.

He was hiding something, and yet, I didn't want any space between us. It felt as if he saw through all the accouterments my mother had demanded be placed on me. He saw through to the real me.

Before I could fully come to terms with how I felt about that, the music finished, magic lights of green, blue, and yellow twirling through the air.

My awareness of the world around us increased. I took a step back, Lonvar's hand easing from mine. I wanted to latch on to it, but instead gave the expected nod after he bowed a bow as deep as he'd given my parents. Heat rose to my cheeks. Before I could say anything, Rumam came bustling over, the woman with him and Herni close behind.

"Well done, sis," he said. "All eyes were on you."

Was that meant as a compliment or a barb? Probably the latter but I wanted to hope for the former.

His partner's smile froze.

I kept my own smile pasted on. Rumam had to know why everyone watched me and tittered behind my back.

"We're all so grateful you've returned to us, Princess." The woman put such emphasis on my title, it sounded like she called me a rat.

"I'm sorry—who are you?" I barely hid the jab behind a soft tone and a fake smile.

She pursed her lips and moved her head slightly as she spoke. "Oh, you wouldn't know me. I was touring different countries, when you returned from your little...moment, but now I'm back. For good." She stroked Rumam's arm as she said that, but I didn't think he noticed. "My name is Hula, of the house of Sask."

The house of. I pffted. No one introduced themselves in that stuffy old way anymore, unless they were showing off. And the way she said *moment,* I knew she was talking about me going to Chardonia like it was a bad thing. "I see."

From the skin tightening below her eyes, it was clear she knew what I meant. For one who thought so mightily of herself, she sure didn't know how to school her emotions. She let out a loud giggle. "Your brother is simply the best."

Rumam grinned, like her words actually mattered to him. Who was this woman? Yes, I knew of her family—the Sasks were a wealthy family from down south—but how had she slunk into my brother's life and what did she plan to do with him?

"And you, Hula, are the second best," he said.

Lonvar wrapped an arm around me, holding me tight. Without knowing why he did it, I was grateful for the added strength. Neither of these two were on my good list. Hula was disdainful and kept tugging at my mind, mixed with something negative I couldn't quite recall. And I had to remember that Rumam was probably leading the tarnished kidnappings.

"Do you mind if I steal her for the next dance?" Rumam asked, and before Lonvar could reply, continued on. "Of course, you don't. Come on, sis."

Rumam pried himself away from Hula with the promise of

more dances later. He took my hand and dragged me to a clear spot.

I liked the feel of Lonvar's hand in mine better, but being with my brother wasn't bad. This way, I could peel away a few more of his layers. I just had to decide where to start.

"How did you meet Hula?" came out.

"She was in court before you left, but you probably don't remember. She wasn't on your list of interesting people, but she's worked hard to become so in your absence."

She'd certainly done something. But wait. Did what he said mean I'd acted *worse* than the flashy show she put on? The thought left me dizzier than the twirl my brother led me through. Thank the magic that I'd been aware enough to go to Chardonia and help. I'd reached a spot where I'd wanted a change, and finding it took me to a far harder place than I'd expected.

I said, "Good for her." It was the only response that came to mind. "She does seem to have gotten in your good graces."

"Mother adores her, as does Father. Herni isn't as certain, but I'm sure you'll both come around. She's very caring."

"Did you like her before I left for Chardonia?"

He gave a slight wince when I said the other country's name, but covered it with a smooth smile. "I didn't get to know her well until we met on one of the journeys Mother sent me and Father on. She has a way with words and influence. She's got Mother's approval."

And that counted for everything in this country. The song was already half over, and I hadn't gotten anything useful out of him. I needed to change the subject toward the information I wanted. "Been out to the mountains lately?"

He gave me a funny look. "With you and the others. Already forgot how amazing a time we've been having?"

Right. It wasn't going to be that easy. "I meant without us."

"I've been too busy to go any other time."

True. He'd been kept in meetings all the time he wasn't with us. He'd stayed late, behind closed doors, with diplomats or members of the court on several nights, doing whatever it was that he did.

He spun me in a circle and pulled me back. "I thought you'd be more fun tonight."

"Sorry." I wasn't. No reason to be fun, after all I'd been through getting my fake persona on for the night. "Guess I'm tired."

"No one's supposed to be tired at a ball." With a quick look around, he leaned closer and whispered, "Don't tell anyone, but I am too."

A laugh escaped me, more joyous than I expected. Who was this man, and what had he done with my brother? I'd seen some of this when we'd spent time together recently, but it was a far cry from the Rumam I knew growing up. "The Crown Prince doesn't show any signs of fatigue."

"The Crown Prince is a fantastic ballgoer." A corner of his mouth lifted and dropped again. "Haven't you been sleeping well? You're in your rooms before I go to bed."

He was having an eye kept on me. It could be because I was tarnished and he wanted to take me into his scheme. If Mila and Lonvar weren't with us, he could have captured me on any of our outings. No, that wasn't true, if he had all those people guarding the tarnished, he could have arranged for something. And it felt like there was a hint of real caring in his words. Best stick to the truth, or as much as I was willing to give. "It's true I haven't been sleeping well."

We went through several paces of the dance quietly. When he spoke, his words were soft. "Is it because of what happened to you?"

The depraver flashed through my thoughts. I shoved him out, but not quick enough to keep myself from stumbling slightly.

Rumam narrowed his eyes at me, before his face brightened. "We should talk of better things. Like where Mother found these musicians. They are subpar with their spells, but the music is good enough."

77

Leave it to him, to focus on the superficial. Or was he doing it to spare me?

As he took me through another twirl, I was left wondering how much he guessed about me and if he was trying to prevent my breaking down in the ballroom, as I felt I might. Someone who thought like that wouldn't hurt the tarnished, would he?

CHAPTER 13

The ball went on well into the night.

I hated that I couldn't leave. My rooms called to me, my bed even more so, but I'd promised Mother I'd stay. I could probably leave before the end, but that time wasn't here yet.

The ballgoers mingled together well for the most part, yet several of them seemed to steer clear of any of the tarnished. Enough of them were here that it was a chore, but not so many that avoiding them was impossible. The other tarnished weren't officially members of court, yet having them here brought more comfort than I expected. If it was my dad who brought them, it was meant as a kind gesture, but I didn't think I or they were feeling that. They huddled together in groups by themselves with only the occasional ballgoer joining them. I didn't know if they were glad to be here or not, but they all held themselves a little stiffly.

My brothers danced with every woman they could—twice with those with massive spell-work done. Rumam danced with Hula more than a handful of times. Lonvar rarely danced with anyone else, but neither did he stay near me. He appeared to be working the crowd as much as my mother did.

I wished I knew why.

Dad came up beside me with a sigh.

"Tired?" I asked.

"It's a late night for an old man like me."

If we weren't in a public place, I would have pulled him in for a hug. "You're anything but old."

"I feel my age on nights like this." His gaze followed my mother, as she sparkled through the crowd, dress changing from one style and color to the next every so often.

She laughed at something someone said, more carefree than when she looked at me.

Dad asked, "Do you think she's happy?"

My first response was to dismiss him, but I watched her carefully. "She certainly appears so."

"She can be a good actress."

I could agree with that. "Are you worried she's unhappy?"

His answer came out hesitant. "I'm sure it's nothing." He turned toward me. "Why aren't you out, dancing more?"

Excuses came to my mind, but I settled for, "I'm tired too."

"That may be your reason now, but I haven't seen you dance with anyone besides your brothers and that Lonvar."

"You don't like Lonvar?"

"I never said that."

Smiling up at him, aware none of those who watched us was close enough to hear, I said, "Your tone of voice says otherwise."

His eyes glittered. "It's like you never left."

The comment sliced into me. The vain princess of my past was elusive after seeing so much suffering in Chardonia. I would never be that girl again after all I'd been through. I didn't want him to see how much it hurt, so I turned my gaze back on Mother, who was slowly making her way toward us as she spoke with others. "I feel that way sometimes," I said. And it sat heavily in my stomach. Had I learned anything while gone?

Despite my reluctance, Dad's grin widened. "Good. I missed you."

He placed a hand on my shoulder, and I wanted to curl up in

his arms and cry. To tell him everything that had passed, and all the fears that still haunted me. He'd been gone so much, I hadn't gotten the chance. But we were in the middle of a ball. Even if we weren't, Mother had arrived. "Why aren't you two mingling?" she asked in the haughty tone of being the queen.

My grimace only barely stayed in check. "Dad and I were taking a moment to talk."

She sniffed. "You can do that when there aren't people who want to speak with you."

A glance behind her certainly showed looks in my direction, but I didn't think the type of talking those people wanted to do was the sort I wished to join in. Gossip was not on top of my list, especially when I was the one gossiped about. "I'm sorry, Mother. I'm afraid I'm fatigued. I'm not accustomed to long ball nights these days."

Her expression hardened, which she probably only let show because her back was to the room and no one could see it except Dad and me. "Do what you must. The old Tawny was much better at balls, anyway."

She took Dad by the arm and gently walked away, not letting out any of her anger, but I felt it all the same. It stung my tattoos and my scalp under my wig. My body was rigid with emotions I didn't want to name.

I couldn't stay here any longer. Too many people were already talking about me without my making a scene, and a scene was what I wanted to make.

It was a stretch of my patience, to keep a pleasant expression and not run out of the room. Still, I went away as swiftly as I dared, only too grateful when I found the doors leading out onto the balcony. The cool night air stung my skin as I hurried to the side, down a narrow stairwell, and into the garden. As soon as I was out of sight of the doors, I ripped the wig off.

Marching through the high garden bushes felt good. I let some of my anger out as I stamped around, smacking my shoes against the ground.

Footsteps scuffed behind me. Fear smashed into my chest. I swung around and lashed out with the wig.

"Ouch," came the sharp cry of a familiar voice.

I scrunched my eyebrows. "Lonvar?"

"Yes."

I still held my arm out before me, blocking much of my view. I lowered it. "What are you doing out here?"

"Saw you leave, and I was concerned." The shadows fell over his face, hiding his expression.

I huffed, frustration rumbling inside me.

He stepped closer, and the moonlight finally caught his features. His gaze was soft. "I will leave if you wish it."

I wadded the wig into a ball and chucked it as far as I could. As it soared through the air, I growled and let out a bit of bright red magic, hitting the wig in an explosion. Mother wouldn't be happy. I didn't care. "I'm sick of expectations."

"Let's get out of here, then."

I narrowed my eyes. "Are you serious?"

"Yes, if that's what you want."

I studied him. Did he really mean it? We hadn't gone anywhere alone since I first saw the tarnished, but then Mila had been with us. Also, it was late. But with anger and sadness swirling within me, I was tempted.

He reached into his pocket, pulled out a handkerchief, and held it toward me. Instinctively, I knew what he meant, so I didn't hesitate to grab it and use it to scrub the makeup off my face. Certain it was still a mess, I gave it one more go-over. Even if it was smeared, it felt freeing to have my skin and tattoos showing.

"Let me change, and I'll meet you back here," I said. Because getting away from this place with him sounded like exactly what I needed, and I realized I trusted him enough not to take Mila.

I didn't wait for him to answer but hurried to my room. I still had a little makeup smeared across my tattoos, so I cleared it away before changing into dark breeches and a matching blouse. I put on a pair of comfortable shoes, left a note for Mila not to worry about me, and snuck out.

She'd worry anyway, since she was supposed to go with me when I was out of the castle, but I needed some space from this place and its reminders. Even Mila.

Lonvar was right where I'd left him. The moonlight caught his smile as he spotted me, and I grinned back, a rush of giddiness flipping through me. I hadn't snuck off since I was maybe fifteen.

Silently, we left the garden and found his motorcar. I gave a nod to the guards as we went, but doubted they recognized me for who I was. There had been other tarnished at the party, and we all looked the same to them. Hot anger flicked in me, but it wasn't their fault things were the way they were. Though they should have been paying attention to people's faces whatever society said about the tarnished.

We climbed into the motorcar and drove away. The farther we got from the castle, the more the weight that pressed on my spirits lifted.

"Do you want to talk about it?" Lonvar asked after the castle was long gone.

I shrugged. "It's probably treason, to talk about my mother the way I want to."

"There's a difference between venting about your mother and crying sedition from the crown."

"You might be right, but I'm not accustomed to it, all the same." That didn't mean I would remain silent. Lonvar was far too easy to open up to, and it was more difficult to know when to stop than when to start. "As you saw tonight, Mother prefers me to not look like the tarnished I am. She threatened to dismiss my lady's maid if I didn't comply with her wishes."

"That must have been hard."

My eyes burned. "More than I expected." I'd felt fake. So very fake.

He reached for my hand and gave it a squeeze.

The words kept pouring from me, and I was grateful he was

the one here to listen. "I try to do as she wants, but it's never good enough." Even not trying to solve the problem of the tarnished being kidnapped, other than to try and peel the layers off my brothers. It was all too much pressure when I wanted to do more to help. "I just want to forget about things for a while."

"How about we go for ices?" he asked.

"Is anywhere open, this time of night?" I asked.

"Lots of places. Any favorite we should visit?"

My thoughts stretched back to a time before Chardonia. Before my cares grew heavier. "Silpew's, if they're still around."

He turned left. "One of my favorites."

As he drove, my tiredness, anger, frustration, and fears ebbed away. I found myself wanting to bounce in my seat with more than just the bumps in the road. When he came to the ice shop, several other motorcars and horses were waiting outside.

I hopped out of the car, memories rushing back to me and leaving my steps lighter than I could remember them being in a long time.

Lonvar opened the shop door for me, and the light and sounds of happy people rushed out into the night.

I stepped inside, the sweet smell of candy, pastries, and ices filling my nose.

Though we were given a few glances, they were nothing like the odd stares I got at court. We took a table, and a waitress came to take our order. Once I'd picked honey-melon ices and he chose winter berry, she left.

"I haven't ever seen you smile so wide," Lonvar said.

I should stop grinning, but I couldn't seem to make myself. There were several other tarnished in the shop, taking ices and treats, along with Envadi patrons. "It feels good to be almost normal," I said.

He watched me carefully. What was he thinking?

I didn't dare ask.

He said, "Wish it could be like this all the time."

"So do I." I leaned closer. "You never told me—what is it you do for work? Are you really a member of court?"

"What makes you think I'm not?" His expression was unreadable. Frustratingly so.

"You don't act like the rest of them, gossiping and spelling. I'd add partying late into the night, but... Well, here we are."

One corner of his mouth turned upward. "Here we are, indeed."

"So? Courtier or not?" I wanted to push him into answering. As attracted as I was to him, there was more I wished to know.

"I don't think you'll like the answer." His gaze was everywhere but on me.

I wanted to reach across the table and take his hand, but it felt too forward. "Try me."

"If you insist. But don't say I didn't warn you." He looked at me now, eyes serious.

Our ices were delivered, and I dove straight into mine, enjoying the way the slightly sweet and flavored shaved ice crunched between my teeth and melted on my tongue. "Well?"

He used a spoon to pick at his ice but didn't bring any to his mouth. "I'm not a member of court."

"I knew it." I pointed my spoon at him. Realizing how loud I'd been, I quickly quieted myself with another bite. "Sorry, but I thought so. What is it you do, then?"

"It's not something I should tell you."

I pouted. "Why ever not? I'll keep it a secret if you'd like."

His gaze became intense. "You would have to, but no. I can't. There's more than my reputation at stake. Perhaps another time."

Disappointment didn't slide down nearly as well as my ice did—even if I understood him. "I get it. It's different, but there are things I don't like to talk about."

"Thank you for understanding," was what came out of his mouth, but his eyes said something different. Something full of sorrow.

"You'd better not be in on the plot and trying to get me

captured," I shot at him in a whisper, though I doubted he would. He'd had plenty of chances to do so already.

With a sad laugh, he shook his head. "Nothing like that." And this time, he took my hand, his fingers cold from holding his glass of ices. "I promise I'm trying to keep you safe."

"It's a little late for that." And yet, his touch heated more than just my hand. The moment grew long, though it couldn't have been more than a few seconds. I wanted to scoot over and have him sit next to me in the booth, so our legs and arms would be pressed up against each other. "Tell me more about you. About your life. We've spent so much time together, yet there's much I still don't know about you."

"I'm just an average young man, making my way in the world."

I laughed. "I hardly think that's the case. Everything about you speaks of far from average to me. When you were a child, what did you want to be when you grew up?"

"I never wanted to work. I wanted to spend all my time fishing."

I perked up. "I didn't know you liked to fish."

He nodded. "We lived near a lake, and before my father died, we used to go at least once a week. Oftentimes more. My mother still lives in the house I grew up in, and when I get the chance to visit her, I always make a point to go fishing."

"Sounds gloriously peaceful and fun. I've only been fishing once, but there was something thrilling about the tug of a fish on your line."

"I bet you squealed."

I giggled, feeling more carefree than I had in years. "I can't deny it."

"And how did the fish feel about all this racket?"

"I made my dad let it go. I felt so bad about it flopping about. I didn't eat fish for an entire year after that."

He grinned. "I ate nothing but fish for a whole year, once."

"Didn't you tire of it?"

With a shake of his head, he added, "My mom is a good cook.

She'd make fish stew, fried fish, fish soup, grilled fish, and fish more ways than I can remember, despite the fact that I ate them all growing up. She always fussed over me saying I'd turn into a fish if I didn't change up my diet now and then."

"Sounds like you had a happy family life."

"We did." His expression grew solemn, as he used his spoon to twirl his ices around without eating them.

"You don't have to talk about it, but if you do want to—what happened to your dad?"

He sighed and leaned back against his seat. "He worked at the hydroelectric plant."

Made sense, since they lived by a lake and enjoyed being out on it so much.

"About a year and a half ago, there was an accident that took three people's lives. One of them was my dad."

I hadn't heard about that, but it was when I was in Chardonia, so I shouldn't be surprised. Still, my heart ached for him and his mom. What mourning and grief they must have gone through. I held out my hand, for him to take if he wanted. When he slipped his into it, I gave a gentle squeeze. "I can't imagine how difficult that must have been for you. I'm so sorry."

He looked down. "It's still difficult, at times. I wake with this aching feeling in my chest and wonder why, until I remember." His gaze found mine. "I like to fish now because it reminds me of him and all the good times we had together. He would have liked you."

Heat tickled my cheeks. "I would have liked to know him, but I do know he and your mother have raised a good son."

"I try, but sometimes it doesn't feel like enough."

"I get that." I understood so well how that felt... "We simply have to try our best."

"That's what I'm going for. It's been good to help the refugees from Chardonia, but there's obviously still much to do with them."

"Agreed." I wanted to comfort him more. I slid out from my side of the table and slipped in next to him on the bench.

He wrapped an arm around me, and I snuggled into him.

Was I comforting him or the other way around? Perhaps both. "This is nice," I said.

"More than nice." His voice was deep and pulled my gaze up to his.

Our faces were only inches apart. My breath caught, and I found myself entranced by him. He liked me—that much was clear—but did he like me as a friend or something more? The way his head tilted toward mine, I was inclined to think it was more.

I didn't wait to see if he would finish the journey to my lips. I moved, making my lips collide with his. At first, the kiss was rocky, but then it melded into something sweet and tantalizing, and thoroughly public.

He tasted of sweet berries and summer. Of fun and caring and passion I was just beginning to discover. His fingers brushed against the back of my neck, making me long to deepen the kiss and keep him close.

All too soon, we pulled apart, both breathless.

I was very aware that we were among others. That I, a member of the royal family, probably shouldn't have gone around kissing anyone I wanted. And yet, it didn't matter. I was just another tarnished in the shop, enjoying a stolen moment with the man I was growing to care for.

His lips turned upward, and before I knew what he planned, his mouth was back on mine. I poured myself into the kiss, wanting him to feel all I did. He held me close, like I was treasured and sweeter than he tasted.

His mouth was cool from the ices, but the heat between us grew, drawing me in more. The scent of candy, fresh air, and a deep woodsy scent filled me. He suffused all of me. The taste of sweetness, the feel of heat, the smell that was his, the roughness of our breath mingling—and when I fluttered my lashes, the quick flash of the attractive man I wanted to spend all my time with.

When we pulled apart this time, it was slow and without a care for anything around me. Only him.

The room came back into focus, bringing with it the soft sounds of diners talking and laughing. None of them seemed to care that Lonvar and I had just shared our first kisses.

I was warm and happy, and I didn't want the moment to end.

I settled my head on his shoulder, content to let the moment linger. My cheeks warmed at the thought of how good it felt to give him my lips. I could have stayed there far longer than I should have, but somewhere close by, a fiddle started up, playing a jig that pulled me back into a sitting position.

With a glance up, I found him watching me. I grinned, grateful we were in this together.

I let myself have a minute, but all too soon the reality of the world came crashing in. There were things we had to do, and together, we could accomplish them.

The tarnished. There had to be a plan we could enact. A way for us both to do more, but not only that, to help those who really needed it. "You have to take me in to a tarnished encampment."

He jerked away. "What? *No.* I just said I'm trying to keep you safe. That would be doing the opposite."

"I'm not asking; I'm telling. There's too much going on I don't know about. My brothers aren't giving us any information. My mother might be doing something, but I don't know what. We need more information on what's happening to the tarnished. If you don't help me do this, I swear on the queen, I will act without you and I know you'll like that even worse."

He covered his eyes and groaned. "I knew bringing you in on this was a mistake."

I scoffed. "Not a mistake. The best thing you could have done. We're just not making any progress yet because we've spent too much time cozying up to my brothers. If they really are involved, they're doing a good job of hiding it. They're always either with us or in meetings at the castle." Before he could argue, I added, "They could be meeting with others involved with it, but Mother keeps them incredibly busy—especially Rumam, with preparing him to be king one day. He could be part of it, but we need to look into other options as well."

Lonvar looked up at the ceiling and muttered something that sounded an awful lot like a curse toward me, before relaxing back into his usual posture and taking a bite of ice. "What, exactly, are you suggesting?"

"Simple. You take me in, posing as one of their people who caught a tarnished, and we get as much information as we can gather while there. I'll be a prisoner, and you'll be one of the ruffians. When we're ready to go, you'll say you're supposed to take me and however many others you think we can, and we'll simply walk out of there."

"What if the ruffians all know each other?" he asked.

"It's possible, but what does your information tell you?" I had a feeling he knew far more than he was letting on—I wished he'd let me in on it as well.

He grunted. "They don't all know each other. It's too big an operation."

"All the more reason we'll be able to get in, and that we should do so. Look around you. How many of these tarnished will be taken, if we don't do something about it? And they are only a small fraction of the ones in the country. We have to do something."

"That doesn't mean I have to like it." He grumbled another phrase I couldn't make out under his breath.

"But it means you're going to do it, for the greater good." I hoped I wasn't pushing too hard.

He sighed. "Yes."

"Good. Let me finish my ices, and then we can go make plans to break in later today." Because it was well past midnight.

"You want to go in with no sleep?"

I waved his concern away. "We can nap after we make plans, but the sooner we go in, the sooner we get information, and once that happens, we'll be able to get them out of there." And hopefully avoid too many people looking for me.

He shook his head, but a smile crept its way onto his expression. "You're something else. You know that?"

I gave him my sauciest grin. "I know." But the way he said it left my heart fluttering in my chest. The feeling didn't stay long, as I gulped down the rest of my ices. Today, I would be taken prisoner again. Even if it wasn't real, the thought left my hands shaking and my thoughts stuttering.

CHAPTER 14

Lonvar's home was small but well kept—more so than I expected from a single young man. He tried to offer me the bedroom, but I refused, plunking down on his couch instead. It would have been too weird, otherwise. I slept fitfully and not nearly long enough, before I got up and rummaged around his kitchen to make a breakfast of sorts, something I'd learned in Chardonia.

Lonvar stumbled out with dark circles under his eyes, but dressed and ready for the day. "You didn't have to make anything."

"I don't get to very often, anymore, and I enjoy it." I set a plate of eggs and scones in front of him.

"Thank you." He dug in.

I waited until he slowed down, before asking, "Where are we going?"

"There's an encampment south of here. Not far, actually, but enough distance from the city to not be easily stumbled upon. Finding this one took some work, but it'll be our best bet of getting in and out quickly. It's in the woods, but the land is flat and the trees are dense."

"Places for us to run if needed."

"Exactly."

I hoped it didn't come to that. "How many places do you know of, with imprisoned tarnished?"

"After losing the one last week—yes, the place I showed you last week cleared out—we're down to four. We haven't found any that are more than twenty miles from the capital."

There was a lot of information I wanted to talk about there, but I chose to focus on— "You said *we*. Who is *we*?"

He paused with his fork halfway to his mouth. It took a moment, but he returned to eating like he had been before. "You and I, of course."

I narrowed my eyes at him. "If you're not going to tell me the whole story, fine, but don't lie to me."

"Sorry." He did have the decency to look abashed. "I shouldn't talk about it, but you're right. There are others."

A pressure lifted from my chest. Not a lot, but enough to make it easier to breathe. We weren't the only ones who believed it was wrong to treat the tarnished as less than human. "What do you think these people are doing to the tarnished? Does anyone have an idea?"

He shook his head. "We haven't been able to get close enough to figure out what they're doing. It has to do with some sort of machine, but that's all we know. We've been focused on trying to get details about your brother—how he's involved—and how we can get closer. In truth, we only discovered how deep the plot against the tarnished goes two weeks before I showed you. It's been a mad scramble, to find all the encampments and figure out what's going on."

"Do you think it's been happening for a while?"

"Unfortunately, yes. There have been whispers for about a year. It's likely gone on longer."

"A year?" I sat back in my chair. "How could it have gone on so long, without people discovering it?"

"I'm not certain, but it doesn't bode well."

"It must be my brother's involvement. How did learn about it?"

"Without going into too many particulars I can't discuss—a

93

group was overheard talking about it in a bar. They said enough that we could figure out it was actually happening, and find one of the places. Once we knew what was out there, we suspected there might be more, so we widened our search."

"Which means there are likely more places you haven't discovered yet."

He put his fork down, clearly finished with the meal he'd been inhaling just seconds ago.

I almost felt bad for making him lose his appetite, but this was an important matter. I should have thought to ask for these details when we first escaped from the encampment he showed me.

He stood, grabbed his dishes and went to clean them off.

Together, we made short work of the dishes. I didn't know about him, but I was stalling. Yes, I wanted to go and help, but fear of what could happen clutched at me, slowing my movements.

I said, "We should get going."

"Let me grab my gun." He went in his room and came back, tucking the gun into the front of his breeches. "The other ruffians had them, so I won't be out of place should they find it. We can use magic if we need to too, you're strong with it."

I tilted my head to the side. "I haven't done that many spells around you. How do you know how powerful they are?"

He turned pink, but I couldn't figure out why. "I know you're strong, from all the spells you did before you left. The balls and parties you attended were proof enough."

Why was he embarrassed about the statement?

"How did you know I could turn those vain, useless things into spells that would work in a fight?" I asked.

"Because you were in Chardonia when it was overthrown."

I didn't want to admit how I'd only done vain spells before I left, but he was correct. Oh, I knew some defensive spells before I left. Attack ones too. But nothing like I did after going to Chardonia and practicing spells that would bring down those ruling the country unfairly.

"Shall we?" He swept out his arm toward the door.

94

I went out, and after he locked up, we found a messenger to send to the castle that I was well, just out and about. I contemplated telling them what I was doing in case things went bad, but I couldn't have them storming in and ruining the hard work of Lonvar and his collaborators. Worse, they might not come at all. We both got in his motorcar. The drive was quieter than I would have liked. Tense.

It was hard enough to think about what was coming without the silence, but I didn't know how to detract from my worry.

The best I could try was, "Are you going to bring the motorcar, or are we walking in?"

"Driving in."

"Do you need to tie me up or something, then? It doesn't seem like the type of thing I'd come along willingly to." It wasn't that I wanted to be bound, but we had to be smart about this if they were to believe us.

"Good point. I have some rope. The kidnappers probably have magic-canceling ones, but this will do for our purposes."

"And you can shove me in the back seat."

He grunted. "I still don't like this plan."

"But we don't have a better one. We need information, and I'm the best person to get you in there."

"I know. I just don't like it." He pulled the motorcar to a stop. "Stay here."

"Where are you going?"

"I need to talk to someone. I'll be back in a moment." He gave me what was probably supposed to be a reassuring smile, but it looked too forced.

He didn't go in the house, like I expected, but instead went down an alleyway. Maybe I should follow him.

I sat with indecision, fingers wrapped around the doorhandle. Following him could be a good way to figure out more about who he was working with. He had to be keeping them secret for some purpose, but it didn't stop my curiosity.

Before I could decide, he came back around the corner, some

of the stress lines on his face smoothed out. He hopped back in, and we took off down the road.

"Good news?" I wanted to pry information out of him, but how?

"Not bad news."

I bit my bottom lip.

He reached over with his right hand and grabbed my left one, while keeping his gaze on the road. The touch soothed me with its warmth and comfort.

"You're right," he said. "This is the best thing to do. We'll both gather what information we can, and then get out of there."

I nodded, grateful for his hand in mine, yet cautious not to squeeze as hard as I wanted to. When he'd shift, he would move my hand with his, and I stayed with him as he put in a different gear. We went south of the city as I clung to him. We were silent, but this time it wasn't as tense. Worry still hung in the air, but with him near, it was bearable.

After we'd driven for around an hour, twisting and turning down unfamiliar roads, Lonvar pulled off to the side. "Almost there. We'll get you ready to go here, before we continue on."

Without a word, I got out of the car and climbed in the back seat. It was cold and unfamiliar. He got in beside me, rope in hand from grabbing it off the floor as he came in. I held out my hands to him, though I'd rather have told him I changed my mind.

He hesitated, before wrapping the rope around my wrists. "Sorry. I'll leave it loose enough that you can get out, while still making it convincing."

"It'll be worth it."

"You're shaking." He finished off the knot and took my hands. "Are you sur—"

"Don't ask. I don't want to change my mind." I did linger, and he didn't seem any more inclined to move.

"You're brave for doing this," he said.

"Or insane."

He shrugged. "Maybe, but insanity and bravery often lie close together."

His words warmed me enough that the shaking eased. He was so close, and he was kind and thoughtful. I wanted to lean into him and feel his arm wrapped around me. To tilt my head toward his.

But no. That was the wrong type of thinking for a moment like this. I had to get my head on straight, if we were going to move forward with our plan. I pulled away from him, but gave a smile so he knew I wasn't upset—far from it.

He must have tried to smile back, but it came out as a wince.

Once he was in the front seat and we were going again, fear trickled through me at what we were about to do. We had to go forward with this. Had to move on and figure out how to save the tarnished.

And yet, the stuttering anxiety in my stomach said it wasn't going to be easy.

CHAPTER 15

The tarnished came into view around the trees, other men and women surrounding them as they sat on the ground. The clothes the tarnished wore ranged from fancier, night-on-the-town apparel, to shabbier work outfits. All were dirty and some were torn. Their expressions were downcast, dejected. The groups of tarnished tied to trunks went into a densely wooded area, tents off to one side, probably for the kidnappers. There were about ten guards scattered about them with guns at their hips, and—no doubt—magic of their own.

A tied-up woman jerked back from the nearest guard.

He spat at her.

Hot rage and icy terror splashed through me in alternating currents that left me dizzy.

Lonvar pulled the motorcar to a stop next to several others, hopped out, and pulled me out of the back. I pretended to struggle, and he yanked me backward so my back was against his front, my hands tied behind me with him holding the rope. Despite appearances, my muscles were less tense with him by me.

We moved closer to the group, but none of them paid much attention to us, probably because they were used to such sights.

98

That was good. It mean Lonvar should be able to move about easily enough.

My thoughts flashed to my family. They probably didn't realize I was missing, especially after I'd told them not to worry. But if things went wrong...

No. We wouldn't let things head that way.

"This is the stupidest idea you've ever had," Lonvar hissed.

"Shut up. They'll notice something's off," I said over my shoulder. They might realize that anyway, but I wouldn't make it easy on them. I couldn't help but add, "I've had stupider."

He grunted and jostled me forward. I tripped over a rock and headed toward the ground face first, but he righted me before I landed. The kidnappers finally looked toward us. Two of them came toward us—a man and a woman. They were similar enough in features that they could be brother and sister. Dark hair, dark eyes, and mouths twisted in a snarl.

She said, "Didn't know any more were coming in today."

"Got this one unexpectedly." Lonvar made his voice deeper and raspy.

The woman scowled at me. "Has she been tested?"

For what? Sweat broke out on my skin, and I couldn't help bucking against Lonvar, who held me tightly, moving his hand to my upper left arm. It eased some of my wildness, but the frenzy to get out clawed at me.

"Got spirit, this one. You can see it in her eyes." The man leered, making me shiver.

"No, she hasn't been tested," Lonvar said.

I hoped that was the right choice. Without knowing more of what they were talking about or doing, I was worried every step would be the wrong one.

"Bring her over here." The woman turned and headed toward the other tarnished.

They cowered on the ground, eyes downcast and hands tied together. Their haunted expressions took me straight back to Chardonia. To becoming tarnished. To the depraver.

99

I bucked again, this time not holding back my fear.

Lonvar was gentle with his hands, but his words came out harsh in my ear. "Give up. You're going to have to deal with this."

"Need me to take her from you?" the man asked.

I recoiled away from him, his laughter already haunting my nightmares.

"Nah. I've got her." To me, Lonvar said, "Stupid thing, you're going to get it if you don't stop fighting me."

I simpered. I didn't want to make things worse for him or for myself, but the heat and rage boiled below the surface, ready to kick anyone else that got too close. Maybe this wasn't my stupidest idea, but it was in the top five.

"Right here," the woman said, lips turned up in a mocking grin.

There, waiting, was a large rock with instruments on it that made me recoil. They couldn't tarnish me any more than I already had been, but with tools like these...

A ripple of horror moved through me in waves.

Behind me, Lonvar stiffened, as I bumped up against him. He didn't like this any more than I did, but I couldn't think of a way around it.

My thoughts clamored, bursting inside my skull and screaming at me to run. I shook my head, a shuddering breath escaping me.

Vivid, yellow light swished out of the woman's hands. The spell whipped toward me. It stabbed me in the arm, and then guided my blood through the air toward the man. I barely noticed a second yellow spell with a tinge of blue patching up my arm.

The man cast his own spell—a lush red that made my stomach churn—and used it to enclose my blood in the space before us. There wasn't much, but enough to make me want to scream at them to leave me alone. His studying my life source felt so personal... The violation of it, the indignity, the fear—it all clamored up inside, aching to get free with magic and fists.

I grappled with the emotions, struggling to keep them where they wouldn't get me backhanded like I had been my first days of being a tarnished and forced into servitude. Even during all that time, no one had ever tested my blood for magic.

The man practically drooled, as he stared my blood down, held still by his magic. I eased toward Lonvar, using his proximity to lend me strength and ground me back in the present.

"Strong, this one. Must have done something naughty, to get tarnished, with all this magic in her blood." The man leaned in closer.

I shuddered, and Lonvar ripped me back before the man could touch me. "Where would you like her?" Lonvar asked.

"Magic like that will fetch a hefty price. Put her up front with the others of strong magic." The man pointed toward the area farthest from us, where the tarnished were tied to a tree.

I took a step back, but Lonvar pushed me forward, bracing me with his hands. "You heard him."

I went without a fight. I couldn't ruin this for either of us; we were finally getting answers.

Magic. That was what they wanted from the tarnished. It didn't make sense. Or maybe it did. Tarnished often became so because they had too little magic. Sometimes, women were tarnished because their men tired of them or wished to punish them and not have them in their households any longer.

There were so many tarnished here, it must not matter to the people in charge that it would take more tarnished to get however much they wanted—however it was they were using us for our magic. Most didn't see us as people, so what did it matter if it took a hundred of us to get the magic they wanted?

But what did they want it for?

Lonvar didn't link me to the tree, like the other captives, but loosely tied my rope to theirs. No doubt the guards would add me to those more confined if they realized this, so I sat against the trunk, ready to run if I needed but pretending I was just as incapacitated as the other captives were.

He rejoined the others where they kept watch over all the tarnished. Some of the men and women with guns—and probably magic too—stood in a loose circle, but most were gathered close to where we came in. Lonvar joined those by where we entered. I hoped he was able to get answers from them. No matter what he found, I needed answers of my own.

There must have been a good hundred of us, all together, but divided in smaller groups. I'd been so focused on myself and what was to come, I hadn't paid enough attention to how many of us there actually were. Now, I was more sickened than ever. Whoever was behind this was evil.

If I could only find out who and why. The latter didn't matter as much, but I still wanted to know. To my left was a woman, her eyes closed, as she leaned against the trunk. The lines by her mouth and forehead spoke of many years. Her aged hands were twisted, covered with spots and more wrinkles. I didn't have the heart to disturb her when she probably needed the rest.

On my left was a man, maybe ten or so years older than me, but careworn. His gaze, focused off in the distance. Tarnished men were *always* tarnished because they possessed no or little magic. How did this man come to have enough of it to be placed in the highest-magic-powered group, if that was the case?

I whispered to him, "What are they going to do to us?"

He continued to stare far away.

"He won't respond," said the woman who only moments ago appeared to be sleeping. "I don't know if he was like this before they captured him or only after, but I haven't been able to get a single word from him."

The boiling heat inside me raged. This was wrong. So very wrong. I had to help, but to do so, I needed more answers than I had. "Do you know what they're going to do to us?"

She studied me with dark gray eyes that spoke of too many harsh years. Finally, she settled back against the tree again and whispered, "You don't want to know."

"Not knowing is worse than all I can imagine."

"We might as well be back in Chardonia." Her voice cracked on the last word, showing her brave façade for what it truly was.

I wanted to grip her hand and tell her everything would be well—that Lonvar and I were here to help, no matter what it took —but I was supposed to be tied well enough that I couldn't do so. "Please, tell me. I'd prefer to deal with facts. Are we to be servants for households?"

Her voice came out small. "I'd much prefer being less than a shadow to this."

I was shaking. "What are they doing?"

Her gaze found mine again, but the hollowness there left me colder than the chilled air should have. "They're sucking the magic out of us."

CHAPTER 16

Horror and revulsion shook me. My stomach churned, only my throat's tightening keeping me from losing my breakfast that seemed so long ago. "They're sucking magic from tarnished?"

"I told you that you wouldn't want to know."

As much as I didn't want to hear it, I needed to. It was one thing to use magic from the tarnished, quite another to steal magic and our very lives, to suck the magic out of us. "That can't be. Tarnished have such little magic."

"Not as little as you'd think, but even when we do, those in charge of the encampments have to get the magic from somewhere. Why not a bunch of tarnished?"

"Because it's wrong. And stupid."

"Maybe to us, but they just want to power their spells. Rumor has it, all this magic is going to the upper class," the woman said.

Images of all my childhood up until I left for Chardonia passed through my mind. Balls with spells everywhere. Parties with magic abounding. The frivolity of it. And I didn't just contribute to it, but also encouraged it.

How could I have not seen what problems I was helping create, supporting the push for more and more and more spells

104

and magic? There was a limit to it all depending on how much magic was in one's blood, and it took time to recharge once that limit was reached. Instead of backing off when they hit that limit, someone had the idea to use people as a source of magic. They had gone after the most vulnerable group.

I felt green with sickness and stress. What had I done by not fighting for the tarnished more?

"This is reprehensible." And I had to admit my part in it. "Tarnished should never be treated like this."

She frowned. "We're expendable. Even here, in Envado, we're worth less than shadows. There's no one to care, if all the tarnished go missing. No one at all."

"I care." My voice came out louder than I intended, but none of the guards came rushing over.

She snorted. "And what are you going to do about it?"

Good question. I had to do something. Sitting here, pretending to be captured like them was a start, but there had to be more I could do. Something to get this all to stop. Mother hadn't believed me. Dad might, but he held little real power. My brothers would be my next choice, but if they were truly behind this, it left it up to me to figure out how to use my power to end this. It'd put me in danger, but I'd done that anyway.

One thing I could start with, and that was knowledge. "Tell me everything you know."

Her eyebrows knitted together. "All right, but I don't see what difference it will make."

I wanted to tell her I'd get her out of this, but it wasn't a promise I was certain I could keep—at least not today. There was one thing I could say. "I have hope for a better future."

"You're confident, for someone who's been captured."

I shrugged. "What do you know? Do you have a clue as to who's in charge of the whole operation?" It was probably my brothers, but I didn't want to blame them to their faces without proof. That, and recently, I was almost fond of them.

"No one knows. Even the guards seem not to."

I grunted. That wasn't helpful. And how did Lonvar know? "How do they take your magic?"

"Through our blood. How else?" She seemed worn and tired.

It should have been obvious, but somehow it wasn't. "Does that mean we're going to be like those machines in Chardonia, that charged the power plants?"

"I hate to break it to you, but that would probably be preferable. At least those people used for machines in Chardonia still had a chance at life if they weren't drained dry before they were rescued. Us, they take outright and siphon our blood magic away until we're drained dry."

"They're killing all the tarnished?"

"Don't look so surprised. Turns out Envado isn't any better than Chardonia, despite their pretty words and ways."

I closed my gaping mouth with a snap. "How do you know this?"

She shrugged. "The guards talk."

"Where do they siphon the magic? Where are the—" I gulped. "Bodies?"

"Here once a week, sometimes more. Those they murder are taken away, I'm not certain where, but I heard something about a pit."

I choked on the rising bile in my throat. There had to be something I could do, sooner rather than later. A glance around showed me the guards looked bored but still had their hands on their guns. The group Lonvar spoke with were laughing about something. How could everyone be so cavalier about killing people?

I must have spoken the last sentence out loud, because she answered with a, "We're not people. Remember?"

I looked her straight in the eye. "We *are* people. Taking away our hair, inking our faces, and turning us barren, does *not* make us any less of a person than anyone else."

Her gaze softened. "You truly are naive, aren't you?"

I gaped.

"Didn't you know even the tarnished princess is considered less than a person? No one cares about the common folk who escaped Chardonia."

My heart stumbled over the thought of others believing me to be less than what I was. But I couldn't focus on myself. Doing so was part of what had gotten me into this mess. I'd been so immersed in my own problems, I'd forgotten to stop and think of others. "Refugees are supposed to be taken care of."

"Perhaps on paper, but in the real world, it doesn't happen. I tried to get attention for the rapidly growing number of missing tarnished for months, with no one listening. After I got taken last week, everyone was probably glad to have one fewer tarnished to listen to complaints from."

This wasn't the information I thought I'd gain from her, but they were the words I needed to hear. I gripped her arm, my rope moving away from the tree as I wrapped my hands around her forearm. "You should have never been treated like that. There are people who care."

"Then, where are they?"

Here. I choked down my response. That would matter little to her. My next thought was to tell her of Lorvar, but I couldn't out him. She might be on our side, but I was worried she'd accidentally let the other guards know who he was.

I floundered to find a person—any other person—who I could tell her cared, but there was no one. Mother wouldn't take kindly to my interfering, but she was trying. Perhaps she would do something, but I didn't know if telling this woman that would be a good idea.

Her gaze grew downcast, and she pulled free from my loosening grip. "Like I said, no one cares. How did you get loose anyway?" she whispered.

I shrugged. "I can untie you if you'd like."

"What good would it do? There's too many guards, and I'm too weak with hunger to even try an escape."

I bit my lip. There would be a chance to show her I could make a difference, but I needed more information first. "When did you last eat?"

"Before here. Why feed us when they're just going to kill us in the coming days? They give us water and trips to the outhouse, but that's it."

This had to stop. The sooner, the better. "Do they keep bringing more in? Where do they find us? How do they take us?"

She shrugged. "How did they take you? Tarnished just kept disappearing, until one day, someone knocked me out, and next thing I knew, I was in a car, on the way here."

I ignored her question. "Where did you live?"

"The refugee part of the capital. It's where most of us are. Weren't you there?"

"I... uh... No. I lived somewhere else."

She scrunched her nose. "You live in one of the fancier places in town?"

"Just here and there." I hated lying, but that was partly true. Before I'd come home, I'd been living all over the place.

"If we weren't trapped here, I would insist on you coming with me, to find a place and a job. Too many tarnished wander about, not finding help. Should have stayed in Chardonia. From what I hear at least, things are changing there."

"Yes, they are." My response came out sad. It took me a moment, but I realized it was because I'd rather be there still, helping the tarnished yet living my life.

One woman I'd helped had been a tarnished for over twenty years. I still remembered the haunted look in her eyes when I first started coaxing her into the society. Saying it'd been a challenge was an understatement. She'd shied at every chance—until I'd introduced her to a girl of no more than five, who needed someone to take care of her. The child had lost both of her parents in the fight against the Grand Chancellor, and she and the woman hit it off so quickly, neither minding their outward differences, as they found an inner connection between them.

The memory was warm and comforting. Here, I'd been trying,

but my efforts were mixed in with my mother's wishes and the expectations of others. The weight bore down on me even now.

She sighed, leaning her head back on the tree. "I wish I could offer you something, but there's nothing left here but despair."

Whoever was behind this, a lot of hands were at work in helping make it happen. It could be my brother plotting this all, but if not, then who? There were bad people in Envado. I knew that. There were others who wouldn't mind selling tarnished magic for money. The darkest of criminals.

If it wasn't a known criminal leading the bad people, there had to be someone else, and though it might be my brother...

That woman I'd seen with the tarnished the first time. She'd been so familiar, but I still couldn't place her. Whoever she might be, perhaps she worked with the person behind this all. Why did she seem familiar? If I could figure that out, it would go a long ways to answering my questions.

Help. That's what Lonvar and I should work toward. I needed to change the opinion of so many, starting with my own. I couldn't continue hiding my true self no matter what society and my mother thought. The tarnished deserved more than that.

CHAPTER 17

I spoke with her off and on for a couple hours, not much changing. By the time the sun stretched across the sky had reached its peak, I was hungry, tired, and irritable. Mostly the latter. I wished we could break everyone out of this encampment now, but with so many armed guards, it was an impossibility.

Trying to appear like I was casually looking around, I searched for Lonvar. During my time here, I'd lost track of him. Those gathered by the front had dispersed a while ago, and I hadn't seen where he'd gone. He wouldn't leave me—that, I was sure of—but I didn't like it.

A man came around with a jug of water and passed it around to the prisoners. I took a gulp when he got to me, but he ripped it away before I could drink more. Just as well. Leave it for those who wouldn't get out of here as soon as I would. Except, as I watched, I realized he was doing the same to the others. I wanted to smack him.

Once he was gone, I asked, "Is it always that fast?"

"You get used to it," the woman at my side said.

"How long have you been here?"

"For how much magic I have and how long ago I was taken, I'm well past due for being drained."

I gulped down my fear for her. There had to be a way to get her out of here. To get them all out.

She continued without my prompting. "I think it's been three or four days. They start to meld together."

Only three or four days? If she was in danger after that short a period of time, it would be best to help her escape. Maybe, if I started working on her ropes, I could untie the others and when there was a chance, we could all run.

I glanced at her, trying to gauge how well she'd take the news, when the snap of a branch sounded behind me. When I turned to look, Lonvar was heading toward me. Panic warred with gratitude that he hadn't forgotten me. There was too much to do still, for it to be time for us to go. I should have thought of freeing the woman sooner instead of getting lost in our conversation.

He leaned over me and whispered, "Time to go."

"We have to free the others."

"No time. They're growing suspicious."

"But I need to—"

"Go," the woman said next to me. "Let him take you and do what you can for us."

I gaped at her.

"Quickly now. You'll figure this out and rescue who you can."

"But how did you know that's what we were trying to do?"

She smiled sadly.

Lonvar grabbed my arm and hauled me to my feet. I stumbled, and he caught me, hands sure against my arm. There was so much I wanted to say. I needed to argue and fight—these people needed to come with us—but deep in my bones, I knew that trying to save them would only end in both me and Lonvar being captured. There was no way for us to take on all these guards and get the people out of here.

I glanced back at the woman who sat much like I saw her

when I first arrived, head back against the tree with her eyes closed. I hoped I saw her again.

As we crossed encampment toward where we'd left the car, I tried to watch the guards without looking like I was doing so. They remained disinterested in us, which allowed me to observe them more closely. It couldn't be normal for a guard to take a tarnished away—unless perhaps that tarnished was going to be killed.

I wanted to snarl at all of them, but I kept my head down like I was beat down. I was, but not in the way they'd suspect. More like tore apart by all that was happening to my fellow tarnished just for magic.

We passed the last group of tarnished, and I risked a glance behind. There were more people here than it appeared upon arrival. The hundred or so men and women tied to trees along the way made me yearn to go back, but Lonvar kept me moving forward.

When we turned toward the motorcars, I was shaking. Anger coursed through my muscles, coming out in the only way it could at the moment.

"Where do you think you're going?" a woman's voice called from behind us.

I wanted to turn and snarl at her, but followed Lonvar's lead and ignored her.

Her voice grew louder. "Excuse me. Where are you taking the tarnished?"

Lonvar's hand tensed on my arm. He muttered to me, "Get ready to run."

"And get a bullet in the back?" No, thank you.

"It's the only way we're getting out of here. If it comes to a fight, they've got us in numbers."

"But not in my skills. I trained and fought in a real war; they haven't."

The motorcar was just up ahead, about twenty paces away. So close, yet unreachable. As much as I wanted to put on a burst of speed like he requested, I held myself steady and took another step.

A gun cocked behind us. "Don't take a step farther with that tarnished, or I'll shoot you in the back."

Not waiting for Lonvar to run for it and lose his life, I whipped around and blasted out a shield spell. It was bright yellow and dark green, full of fear and determination. I would get this right. I poured my magic into it, using the knowledge I gained in Chardonia to strengthen it.

A gun blasted off, and through the light of the spell, I saw the woman's gun smoking, but nothing hit either Lonvar or me. I had to hope the spell would hold.

Other guards were rushing toward us.

Lonvar grabbed me by the arm, flipped me around, and pushed me toward the motorcar.

Taking the hint, I put on a burst of speed as my long legs stretched out. Only, we weren't in Chardonia. Most here had long legs, and the guards would catch up to us quickly. My spell wouldn't hold back a human, only attacks coming through as spells or bullets.

I reached the motorcar as shouts from behind grew closer.

They had to be near the barrier now. I ripped the door open and jumped inside, as Lonvar did. I hadn't even managed to close the door, when he started the car.

He put it in reverse, cursing. "Should have parked facing the other way."

We whirled around, and he'd just put it into gear when a body crashed onto the back.

Lonvar slammed his foot down on the gas, as I finally managed to get the door closed.

We burst forward, with the guards crying out.

"Get in your motorcars."

"Don't let them escape."

"Kill the man, keep the tarnished."

I'd been so worried about the tarnished's lives that I hadn't stopped to think about the very real danger Lonvar put himself in.

We were headed down the road, when the revving of other engines came from behind us. I had to hope Lonvar's motorcar was faster. A hand punched through my open window. I ducked before it knocked into me, escaping by a finger's width. The man who crashed into the back—I'd forgotten about him.

He gripped on to the vehicle with one arm, and with the other, he grabbed for me again. I ducked, banging into the gear shifter.

The engine made a terrible groaning sound, and Lonvar cursed again.

I shoved myself, away from the gear shifter and toward the man. Holding out my hands, I struck with the first spell I thought of at him.

"What?" The man blinked rapidly, probably attempting to get rid of the sparkles I'd sent at his face, blocking his vision.

Not waiting for him to recover, I grabbed on to the hand keeping him on the vehicle, and attempted to pry his fingers off. He swung out with his other hand toward me, grasping like he was trying to grip my hair. Grateful I was bald, I head-butted his hand and kept working on his fingers.

"Get rid of him," Lonvar called out.

"I'm trying." Blasted man should let me do the driving next time, and he could do the fighting.

I needed another approach. As we bounced down the dirt road, I worked with only one hand to pry his fingers up, and with the other, I gave a quick jab to his ribs. With a cry, he curled in on himself. His grip loosened enough for me to push him off. He fell to the ground with a *thud* and rolled away from the road.

I trailed him with my gaze, until I saw the others.

Five vehicles drove after us and must have been the reason Lonvar was so intent on getting the man off. We needed fewer distractions in the car, so Lonvar could focus on the road and not on everything else.

"How do I help?" I asked.

He grunted, shifting gears again.

I whirled around in my seat and stuck my head out the window, to get a better look than the small back window afforded. A fraction of a moment later, a hand gripped my blouse and yanked me backward. I tumbled into the seat, just as several shots were fired.

"Are you trying to get yourself killed?" Lonvar yelled.

"I'm trying to figure out how to stop them from following us." I was angry and put the emotion in my words, only I wasn't upset with him or even me. I was furious with the people attacking us. They said to keep me alive, yet the bullets had been real. I could only hope that, with so many of the guards following us, the tarnished would have a chance to get away.

"Figure it out without sticking your head out the window. In fact, duck down. They're getting ready to fire again." Lonvar ducked too, keeping his eyes just barely above the steering wheel.

I scrambled down to where my feet usually went, tucking myself in tight. Shots were fired, one right after another, and sank their way into the motorcar. With each one, I cringed and made myself a little smaller. Curled in a little more tightly.

Another one blasted out.

I gritted my teeth. How would we get out of this?

Lonvar cried out, "I'm hit."

CHAPTER 18

"Where?" If Lonvar was shot, we had to lose our pursuers. *Now.*

"Left arm."

I peeked over, even as more bullets came whizzing past, but didn't see any blood. "I'll stop this."

"Tawny, no. *Wait.*"

But I was up before he could stop me. The windshield shattered with another bullet, unable to take any more direct hits. The good news was that the back shattered at some point too, so I had a clear line to the cars behind us.

I sent a blast of light, bright as I could make it and sparkling. It trailed behind us, hopefully blinding the drivers and shooters. "Weave the car across the road but don't go all the way out."

Bracing myself on the back of the seat, I kept my hand up and the spell going and steady, even as the car wasn't. Lonvar followed my orders a little too well, jerking the vehicle back and forth, but it was enough that the bullets went wide, and only one passed through the car.

"Turn coming," he called out.

I wrapped my free arm around the chair, so as to stay upright, with my hand pushing the blazing-white light

116

streaked with my fear in yellows. The motorcar took a sharp turn, and I slid to the side despite my holding on to the chair. We bounced hard once and reached a smoother road. We still jostled about, though the way was much less bumpy and rocky now.

After making sure my spell was still in place and no one had been able to drive on this side of it, I sneaked a peek in front of us. We were still in the countryside, a long way off from help. Luckily, I knew some healing magic. If only we could stop, so I'd have a chance to use it.

Lonvar shifted gears, pushing the motorcar harder. The air tore at me as it flashed past, making my eyes sting.

"Do I dare put the spell down, to see if they're still there?" I asked.

"They won't let us go so easily."

"That wasn't easy," I grumbled but forced my attention back behind us.

I couldn't see anyone, but a few more shots went off. None came near the car, but they were loud and frighteningly persistent. "How close do you think they are?"

He shook his head, face pale.

"Need me to drive?"

"Yes, but we need your spell more. Turn."

I wrapped my arm around the seat again, as we whipped around another corner. Once I was righted, I pulled the spell closer to our car. In case we were making headway, they'd have less of a trail to follow. I couldn't say it brought me any comfort, but the thick forest around the road helped.

We turned twice more, Lonvar growing paler each time. I had to trade him and get us to safety. "I don't care if they're behind us. Move over."

It was a point to how much pain he was feeling that he didn't protest. "Grab the steering wheel."

I couldn't concentrate on keeping up the spell while switching seats in the motorcar. Afraid of what I'd see when I let it go, I didn't look back to see who was still behind us. I grabbed the wheel and kept my gaze on the road.

Lonvar moved toward me with a grunt, and the vehicle slowed. I maneuvered over him, as he slid into my seat, blood dripping from his arm.

Fear for him sluiced through me, but there was no time to do anything about it. I put my foot on the gas, fixed the gear, and chanced a glance in my side mirror. Behind us, there was only one car, and it was far enough that they weren't shooting, but they were gaining.

"Hold on." I put all those years I spent riding fast and carefree to use into getting away from the kidnappers. We flew down the road, bumping and jostling with the speed but holding steady. I slowed just enough to make a turn, the vehicle tilting slightly to my side.

"Don't kill us," Lonvar shouted, but more weakly than I would have liked. "It'll do no good, getting away fast, if you tip us over."

"I'm an expert. Trust me." Though the truth was, I would have been more comfortable if I'd driven his motorcar before. "We'll lose them and survive. How's your arm?"

He'd found or ripped up a strip of cloth and was working on tying it around his wound with one hand.

It was awkward and I wanted to help, but I needed all of my attention on the road, both ahead of and behind me. The pavement had smoothed out after the last turn, enabling me to push faster. The engine whined, but I didn't let up.

Some distance behind us, the pursuers turned the corner, and a bright spell came flashing at us. Whatever it was, I wasn't about to let it hit.

I hit the break and swerved off the road. Lonvar yelped. Was it in fear or pain? The spell passed us in angry reds, with purples and greens like a bruise. I eased us back on the road, where the others had gained ground but hadn't yet caught up.

I'd driven a short distance, when another spell came hurtling toward us. I dodged again and twice more, as the spells kept coming, now aiming for the sides or the road as well as the path itself. The weaving in and out the lane made me break out in a sweat.

Another bruise-colored spell sped toward us.

I jerked the wheel as it whizzed by, barely moving out of the way in time. The vehicle rocked with the force I was pushing it on. One more spell went wide, before I turned onto a street that would lead to the city.

"Are they still behind us?" I couldn't handle much more of their antics, and neither could the motorcar. There weren't any more lights flaring toward us, but I was also attempting to keep my sight on the road.

Just before I took another turn, he said, "I don't see anything."

I twisted through the streets of the city several more times, and parked near a busy park. "Let me see your arm."

He covered the wound with his hand, not touching the bandage. "I'll be fine."

"Don't be stupid. I've had training as a healer, so it's something I should be able to help with."

With a scowl and a wince, he moved his hand away from his arm. I got to work right away, carefully peeling the layers of makeshift bandage from around his arm. He hissed as the last of the cloth pulled away from the wound.

It was a clean shot that went through his arm without leaving the bullet in, for me to have to dig out. Also, it'd missed the bone, so that was something to be grateful for.

By the grimace he pulled, it clearly hurt.

I sent a soothing, numbing spell to the wound. It came out in a deep blue with traces of pink. What was the pink about? I'd never had that color in my numbing spells before. I didn't know my own emotions and didn't have time to figure them out.

He slumped back in the seat, his face relaxing. "Did we get away?"

"I think so." I rushed to weave more of my magic because the blood dripped more heavily. I caught it in a spell that guided it back into its rightful place, and took far longer than a practiced healer would, stitching him back together with another spell. "The wound will be sore for a while, unless you take it to a better healer, but it should be good as long as you don't go around exercising it." Because, by the look of his muscles, his clothes had been hiding some good definition.

I shoved my thoughts away from him as a man, and replaced them with others of him as a patient. No matter how hard I pushed, though, the muscle tone on his arm kept returning to me.

My cheeks heated, and I cleared my throat as I sat back. "Yes—well—that should be good to go. Just don't strain it. You're lucky it was a clean shot, otherwise I wouldn't have been able to help much."

"Thank you." He gazed at me with an expression I couldn't—or wouldn't—read.

"It's what partners do. What did you learn?"

He was still pale when he said, "My motorcar will never be the same."

"I beg your pardon. I handled it fantastically. If you'd been left to drive, we would have been caught." When he frowned, I softened my tone and added, "But mostly because of your arm."

He laughed, but it came out weak.

"You'll need some rest and food. No matter how much healing I put into you, those are things I can't replace."

"Drive to the castle, and we'll talk." He leaned back in his seat and closed his eyes, while I started the car up. As I drove, he said, "I couldn't figure out how many more encampments there are, but it sounded like each has about the same number of guards and tarnished as what we saw."

I hissed. "So many? I hope there aren't a lot of encampments."

"More than we'd think from the sound of things."

There were too many evil people in the world.

"They put the magic from the tarnished in a machine which sucks out their magic that they use or sell," he said. "How fast they take the magic depends on how great the request is, and how many machines they get. The balls and parties definitely make the usage go up."

"Blasted Envadi. We're bad countrymen if this is how we act." It wasn't always this way, but over the years I'd been a part of court, every event had gotten more lavish. There had to be a way to get people to see what that lavishness cost, and that cost wasn't tarnished worth nothing, but people. "Even if we break up this operation, unless we change society's thinking, it's going to happen again—with the tarnished or another class of people who can't protect themselves."

He slumped down. "I know."

The rest of the drive was silent, with both of us unfocused.

I pulled through the gates to the castle, driving around toward the castle garage. As soon as I turned the motorcar off, I sagged in my seat. The weight of a country's stupidity sat heavy on my shoulders. At least the Chardonians had been overcome by a few men with lots of power, not an entire class of selfish idiots.

"I should go inside," I said.

"I'll take you." Lonvar reached for the handle.

I shook my head. "I'll go alone. It will give me time to clear my head. Besides, you need to rest."

"Not so much that I can't make sure you're safe."

I snorted. "I'm inside the castle grounds. I'll be fine." I waved at him. "I can handle anyone, even those guards that will be waiting for answers to take my mother, just like I got us away back there."

"You mean when I got shot."

"Yes—well—they won't be shooting in the city. Especially by the castle. Can you drive yourself? Are you feeling up to it?"

"I'm fine. Sore, but nothing that will prevent my returning home."

I nodded. "When should we meet again? How about tomorrow night? Is that long enough to give you a chance to rest? I can snoop around court more, while you heal."

"I hate to say it, but I'll probably need all day. I'll stay in touch via magic messages and will let you know if I can't make it. There have to be options we're not seeing." The dark circles under his eyes were heavy.

I wrapped my fingers around the door handle but didn't open it. "We'll figure this out."

Or die in the process.

CHAPTER 19

Lonvar was scarce the next morning as agreed on, which was what I expected, but I missed him. Rumam even complained about not having him around, but I pretended like I didn't know anything that was going on with him. I'd used the time to deal with arrangements for the upcoming ball and work toward how I could help the tarnished.

My thoughts turned to my partner in adventure a lot, though. Perhaps more than they should. The worry of whether or not he was getting better and resting properly ate at me. I wanted to know he healed like he should, but I also didn't want to bother him. He had sent several notes with vague messages about him healing. It wasn't nearly enough for me.

Worse was the increasingly heavier pressure that I couldn't figure out what to do, how to help the tarnished. There had to be a way to find out where all the groups were, stop them, and change society's opinion. Easy.

Mila knocked and entered with a hideous, puce gown that turned pea green draped in her arms. Another ball tonight. They were far too frequent for my taste, but at least my note had been accepted and my mother hadn't decided to keep a closer eye on me.

Knowing what I did, going to the ball was the last thing I wanted. Yet, it would be one of the few places I could make a difference. Or at least try.

"You can leave it on the bed," I said, as she closed the door behind her. "We need to talk." My worries over what I was about to do threatened to choke me, but I motioned her to the chair next to me anyway.

"Yes, Princess?" She clutched her hands together in front of her in a way that indicated she was nervous, but she was otherwise serene.

Steeling myself for what I didn't want to do, I said, "You have been faithful and loyal for many years. I consider you more friend than lady's maid and guard. Because of that, I've made arrangements for a different position for you."

"What have I done to displease you?" she asked, her expression drawn, before I could continue.

"Nothing at all. It's"—because I didn't want my mother to be able to manipulate me through her again—"what's best for you. I don't want you to lose your job over what I'm going to do tonight and in the future. I've secured a position for you as a lady's maid to another member of court, except she won't have high guarding needs. She's kind and will treat you as you should be treated."

"No."

I leaned back, with a shake of my head. "I'm sorry?"

"Respectfully, Princess, no. I know who this is because of, and I would rather help you through what is to come, even if it means losing my job." Mila held her head high, determination in her eyes.

She couldn't really mean that, but she held my gaze with such confidence, I had to trust she was serious. "But—"

"I'm staying."

I watched her carefully, looking for any sign that she held doubts, but that confident expression and the sisterly love beaming from her made me believe her. "Very well. I'll do what I can to protect you, because I want you to stay, but I can't guarantee anything."

"You don't have to. Is it safe to assume there's no wig for tonight's party?"

"That would be correct."

She grinned. "What do you have in mind?"

"A change of pace."

I was thankful she wanted to stay, and even more so that she'd be here to help me prepare for the night ahead. I wouldn't back down from the challenge I had placed for myself, to change the ways of court and expose the tarnished encampments for what they were.

MOTHER'S SCOWL deepened as I entered the room. "That is not how I instructed Mila to prepare you."

Keeping my head high like Mila had, despite the tremor washing through me, I said, "This is who I am now. No amount of makeup, wigs, fancy dresses, and spells will change that."

She narrowed her eyes. "We'll see about that."

The way she stalked toward me, like a predator moving in for its prey, had me holding up my hands, ready to cast a defensive spell. "Don't make me stop you." Realization struck me hard—I would cast magic against my own mother.

"I am the queen. Nothing can stop me."

I gritted my teeth against my fear and ran the process of a shield spell through my mind. I wouldn't attack her, but neither would I let her do a thing to me.

"Let it be, Mom," Rumam said from behind me.

I didn't turn to look at him, though relief spread through me. Someone else would stand up for me. Out of the corner of my eye, I saw my father with horror etched on his face, his gaze jumping from one of us to the other so fast, he must be growing dizzy.

125

Mother sniffed haughtily. "You know nothing about having a daughter, Rumam."

"Maybe not, but I know my sister, and she's not about to back down. This isn't worth a family fight, especially when we've got a ball to go to."

She thinned her lips, pressing them together so hard that, if it weren't for all the paint on them, they'd be white. "Very well." She turned but added over her shoulder, "No one cares about the tarnished, anyway."

The barb struck me in the heart, clinging there painfully. My own mother was not who I thought she was. I knew she was fond of magic and appearances, but for her to be so against who I was made me want to curl into a ball or lash out. I couldn't decide which to do, so I stood there, with my shaking hands still held out.

Rumam put a hand on my right arm and slowly lowered it, the left following his guidance. Leaning closer, he whispered to me, "She's not worth it."

I gave him a sharp look and whispered back, "Who are you, and what have you done with my brother?"

He shrugged, shook his arms out, and adjusted his suit coat that—while flamboyantly bright blue—didn't hold a single spell. Could he *really* be the one behind the tarnished plot? Doubts bounced about my head, but there was little time to evaluate them, as Herni came to my other side and said in low tones, "We have your back."

Surprise jolted through me. Rumam standing up for me was one thing, but quiet Herni supporting me when he barely spoke to anyone was something else.

To both of them, I said, "Thank you."

Mother led the way toward the ballroom, the doors opened, and someone announced us.

Dad kept glancing at me over his shoulder, with a concerned expression. I didn't want to worry him or raise a barrier between him and Mother, but I wasn't willing to back down, either.

As my brothers escorted me, my tattoos showing, my head bare, and my dress a shade of blue in its elegant simplicity but holding no magic, I felt like the princess I was.

Rumam gave my arm a squeeze and gave a cocky grin.

He couldn't treat me this way and be in charge of the tarnished having their magic stolen along with their lives, could he? It was even more difficult to imagine Herni helping.

I should have spent more time with my brothers before I left for Chardonia. Perhaps then I'd know them better. For that, they'd have had to be around, though.

Before we crossed the doorway, I asked them, "Why weren't you around more while we were growing up?"

Rumam sombered, but before he could respond, we were through the doorway and smiling at those gathered in the hall. It was a larger crowd than usual. Did that have anything to do with my coming to the ball as a tarnished first and then like I'd never gone to Chardonia? Did they want to see what I'd do next, or were they simply here for the entertainment?

Either way, I was happy to see a full crowd. More people meant it was more likely there would be people here to get through to—if I was brave enough to do what was needed. The fact that there were those among the crowd buying their magic through perverse means made me sick, though. There had to be a way to get them to understand.

I caught a glimpse of the wildly brown eyes I'd come to adore looking at, and my smile turned genuine. If nothing else, I'd do my best.

Lonvar's answering grin made me happy I had chosen to come as myself, no matter what it cost me later. And by Mother's reaction, the cost would be great.

Once we were seated on our thrones, the music started. I sat there, my smile more fake, wondering when the best time to strike was. It had to be before people started leaving, but it was still early so not everyone was here yet, despite the size of the crowd. My plans would only work once, because after that,

Mother was bound to have me locked in my rooms. Nothing could interfere with the balls she put on, and I was going to do exactly that.

Lonvar came forward but instead of asking my parents first, like he did last time, he headed straight for me. With a deep bow, he offered his hand. "Would you do me the great honor of the first dance?"

It was out of the norm, but I didn't mind giving him the pleasure. In truth, I wanted him to have it. Him, more than anyone else. I put my hand on his arm, and as we went to the dance floor, the heat of his nearness and warmth of his soul touched me.

I'd fallen for him far harder than I knew. It should have hurt, but instead, I was left feeling better than I had in a long time, maybe ever. Stress and tension would come soon, but for now, I let him glide me along the dance floor.

We weren't the only ones there. Rumam was there with Hula. She shined so bright with spells tonight, it made my eyes hurt to look at her. I didn't know what my brother saw in her, but he appeared quite enamored. I couldn't say I liked her though. Something about her nagged at me, leaving me with a bad taste in my mouth. Whatever it was, I couldn't remember. Maybe I wanted to keep my newly warming-up brother to myself.

I turned my attention back to Lonvar. He was striking, in a simple dark blue suit. It was understated, compared to all the spelled tuxes around the room, the men's clothes as fancy as the women's. Yet, somehow, he made it seem as if everyone else was gaudy.

"You look perfect," I said to him, as his hand cupped the side of my waist and guided me along.

"Only because my joy at seeing you is radiating from me." He laughed. "That was awful."

I joined in. "At least I know you like me."

His expression grew serious, his heated gaze making my breathing come faster. "It's more than that, Tawny. I... That is to say… Well, I've never felt like this before. Ever. I think I love you. No. I know I love you."

A tiny gasp escaped me, before I realized— "I feel the same about you."

Like the first time Lonvar and I danced everyone else around us faded into nothing. The music chimed in my ears in soothing tones. We moved together like we understood each other. I'd known him for such a short time, and yet we'd accomplished so much. I wouldn't have wanted to do all the daring things we'd done with anyone else.

The room snapped back into view and couples twirled around us. I had to tell him. He'd hate it, but he had a right to know. "There's something I should tell you." But I couldn't get the words past my lips.

"Go on." He encouraged me with his gaze, as much as with his words.

I licked my lips. "I'm going to tell everyone here tonight what's been going on with the tarnished."

Panic flew across his expression. "You can't."

Frowning, I pulled away slightly, yet stayed in his arms. "Why not?"

Sweat beaded across his forehead. It was impossible to tell if it was because of our dancing or our conversation. He said, "You just can't."

The song crescendoed, but I didn't move with it. Instead, I stopped where I was and put my hands on my hips, grateful none of the other couples were near us. "Why?"

He muttered, "I never should have brought you into this."

"Excuse me?" My tone grew louder, but I didn't much care.

"Sorry. I didn't mean that. It's just…"

When he didn't continue, I said, "I'm pretty certain you did mean it. So tell me, *it's just* what?"

He rubbed the left side of his face with his palm, like he was trying to obliterate whatever it was he was thinking. "You can't tell anyone what's going on."

"I need a valid reason, and I need it now, because we're drawing attention and I'm going to announce it unless I get a response."

His gaze darted at the crowd forming around us—curious onlookers, who spoke to each other behind gloved hands. I really noticed these people for the first time since stepping in the ballroom. Not only that they were here, but a deeper look.

Something was different. The area still had spells zipping through it, dancing about the air and across the floor in time to the music, but the individuals were different. Most were unlike Hula. They had fewer spells than usual, and what spells had been cast tended to be more subdued.

These people, members of court, some of the lower classes and even tarnished had changed. It was only my preoccupation with what I wanted to do that made me miss it. They were becoming different, even if I didn't know why.

"Look at them," I said. "They're ready to hear the truth. And even if they aren't, I'm ready to give it to them."

I watched him as he took in those around us. Understanding dawned over his features, and his gaze found mine again. "I understand, but there's much at risk if we tell them."

I furrowed my eyebrows as we continued twirling. "What do you mean?"

With a sigh, he said, "I'm a law officer, working as part of a team, to bring down those doing this to the tarnished. It's supposed to be a secret operation, and we only brought you on board when we realized it would give us better access to your brothers. If we tell them now, we will lose our advantage."

We hadn't gotten anything from my brothers, at least not their exact denial, but from their words and actions, I didn't think they were involved. Then the rest of what he said hit me. The secret. The group he was working with. He was a law officer.

CHAPTER 20

"I know," he said, studying me carefully. "I shouldn't have used you like that, but it's my job. I wanted to help those people who've been taken, but I couldn't do that without more information. I was assigned to you because we're about the same age."

I tilted my head in concentration, a memory coming to me. "That first time we met, you were about to leave, when a woman bumped into you."

He reddened. "My boss."

"I see." And I did.

He hung his head. "I'm sorry."

"I understand why you couldn't explain it to me before and why you are now." My voice came out soft. I cleared my throat and straightened. "But they need to know. I'm telling them."

He nodded, yet there was resignation in the slope of his shoulders.

I turned away from him, feeling as if my heart stayed behind with him, wanting anything but to create a chasm between us by going against his duty. If I didn't say this now, if I didn't give these ballgoers the reason to stop their inane actions, they might never change. There was no chance for me to deal with emotions now. I needed to be a royal.

With a serious expression plastered on, I met the gazes of those around us. The murmuring stopped, hands dropping from whispering mouths. Hula glared at me before pasting on a fake smile and latching on to Rumam. My oldest brother gave an encouraging grin. Herni appeared serious, but nodded his head toward me as if in encouragement. My parents hadn't yet looked my way, but I couldn't let that stop me.

People watched with curious eyes, not as wary as I'd expect. Perhaps they were as ready for a change in court as I was.

"Good evening," I said, grateful when my brothers inched their way closer, their gazes on me. I wanted to tell everyone about the tarnished encampments, about those being killed for the ballgoers' frivolity. With what Lonvar said and the changes I saw, even in the short time since my first night back in Envado, I hoped they would listen and learn. "I want to thank you all for coming. The queen puts on spectacular balls, as we're all aware, and I'm grateful you were able to come and enjoy the ball tonight."

In the distance, Mother had on an approving smile.

It wouldn't last long, but I pushed her future disapproval aside and forced myself not to look at her. "Last time you were here, I was dolled up as if I'd never gone to Chardonia," I said. "As if I'd never become a tarnished. Many of you have seen me at my homecoming ball or around town, looking much different. I wanted to say I was wrong to hide my true nature. This is who I am. Who so many of the people who've become Envadi are. We were treated horridly by power-hungry Chardonians. Here, things are often better, but we're still cast aside and unwanted.

"That can't continue. As you've seen me and spent time with me, you *know* I am as worthy to be your princess as I ever was. The same goes for all tarnished. We may look different and have our own challenges to face, but we're the same as you. With your help, I would like to make a better place for the tarnished. Let us bring them into our circles, our homes, our families, and our friendships. When you hear those old Chardonian whispers to ignore us, as if we're less than shadows, remember this moment. We are people too." I looked out among the crowd, drawing my strength together. "And some of us are going missing."

The crowd grew restless. Were my words stirring them, or bringing them discomfort? They should feel them. Their souls pricked with the knowledge, whether they were ready to act on it or not. There'd come a time when they were ready to make friends, but for now, all I needed was more eyes on the situation.

"Tarnished are disappearing in alarming numbers. I need everyone, whether a native Envadi or refugee, to keep an eye out for your fellow mankind." It was on the tip of my tongue to say what was actually happening with the tarnished, but Lonvar being a law officer who sounded like he had a plan, I didn't want to mess that up. I did want more people to be aware, though, so the tarnished were in less danger. "Take care of each other, no matter if they have hair or not or if their faces have been inked or not. We all need to do our part in making certain we help those tarnished who need us."

I gave a sad smile and said, "Please, let me know if you hear of anything and help those who need it."

They looked at each other, shifting in place, and I couldn't bring myself to watch them any longer. To see the true feelings they might have for me after this moment. My brothers grinned at me, making me smile, even if I didn't understand why. They couldn't be behind the plot to steal tarnished magic with that reaction, but then who was?

It had to be someone at court. No one else had as much to gain. Unless some lowlife was gaining off their lust for being the biggest showoff. My gut said the former though.

I let my gaze flitter over the crowd. Which of them was responsible? I forced myself not to glower. It would be the worst move I could make, but I wanted to.

Lonvar was closer, his heat warming my back. I didn't mind. I was a long way from being happy with him—the two of us still had much to talk about—but my feelings for him hadn't changed. He hadn't told me the whole truth, but with good reason. And the darn stirring in my heart mixed with his apology to offer room for hope.

There was a shuffling movement to my right. I turned in time to see the ballgoers parting for my mother, Dad close behind her. He looked tense. Her expression was more carefully cultivated, made to look pleased, for the sake of all those gathered. From knowing her my entire life, I could tell the set of her chin promised trouble.

I continued to project happiness, even as I dreaded the moment I'd be alone with her. She couldn't fault me, for wanting to make Envado a better place, but she could be furious with my breaking the appearance of perfection she'd worked so hard to cultivate in court.

She stopped several steps into the empty area between me and the circle of people. Dad wisely didn't come as near. "Thank you, dear child. That was a pretty speech," she said.

In other words, I wasn't an adult. I was to be patted on the head like a youngster and quickly dismissed. But I wouldn't let that happen. The words needed to be said whether she was *handling* the situation or not. "No, thank *you*, Mother. I learned from the best."

Her lips twitched downward, but her smile was quickly back in place. "Yes—well—let us get back to dancing and enjoying ourselves. I long for a dance." She turned toward my dad and held out a hand.

He took it, and she waved to the musicians with a spell that was nothing more than a bounce of light and flourish. They took the cue and played a lively song, which sent people back to the edges of the room, while the queen and king became the focus of attention.

I moved back with the rest of them, grateful when they let me sneak into their ranks. I wanted to be one of them and to let other tarnished become fully part of our society. My words wouldn't change things overnight, but perhaps some of my actions already had.

As the dance went on, a tarnished woman approached me. She was aged, reminding me of the woman in the encampment I was determined to somehow save, only her face was alight with an inner fire. She didn't waste time waiting for me to speak, as protocol dictated. "As soon as I heard you were tarnished and coming back to Envado, I knew you would do something for us."

Warmth filled me. "There's still much to do, but we're headed in the right direction."

Her smile turned kind, though I didn't know her. "Any help you need, we'll be behind you." She sombered. "There is something I would speak to you of." She glanced to those around us.

What could she have to say? "Go on."

Lowering her voice, she said, "Tarnished are disappearing from my area in the refugee slums as well."

With a sigh, I replied, "Thank you for letting me know. I'm doing everything I can to stop that. For now, don't go out alone. Try to stay in groups." And I needed to do something more so they weren't living in *slums*.

Her eyes widened but then flashed with relief.

"Are there any specifics you know? Anything you can tell me that would help?" I asked.

"If only there was. I've had three friends disappear in the last month. When I reported it, I was told they probably went back home to Chardonia, but I know them. They would never leave, and if they did take that large leap, they would have told me first. We were close. I would have known if something changed their minds or chased them away."

Another thing to deal with. Whoever took these reports needed a good tongue lashing. "If you find out anything more, please send me word or come see me. I will see what I can do about people taking this seriously, but know there are those out there who already are."

I was very aware of Lonvar's proximity. He hadn't left my side,

135

though I hadn't deigned to look at him. He might have lied, but at least, unlike some, he was trying to help.

Still made me angry.

Her words brought me back to the present. "I'll spread the word for tarnished to stay in groups with friends or family."

I should have done this sooner. "Good. We will get through this." I wanted to promise more, that her friends would be found alive and well, but it wasn't something I could guarantee. They might very well have already stolen their magic—their lives.

"Thank you." After I got her name, she left with a curtsy.

The ball continued well into the night. Others came to me to say similar things, but not all who came to me were tarnished themselves. Over half of them were Envadi. Hearing so many left willing to talk to me buoyed me. There was still a chance we'd get through this as a nation, and not revert to evil ways.

It was deep into the night, the ballroom swiftly emptying, when Lonvar—who hadn't left my side despite my ignoring him— whispered in my ear, "I would like to speak to you alone, if you will permit it."

With a nod, I headed out to the gardens, knowing he would follow.

CHAPTER 21

Once we were in the middle of the gardens, secluded in a corner lit bright by the full moon, I finally looked at him. "It must have been difficult, being a law officer and not able to say anything."

"It was hard, and I hope you can forgive me."

I leaned forward, resting my forehead against his. "Done. You did what was needed even though I don't like being kept in the dark."

His arms encircled me, comforting me far more than I would have thought possible. We stood like that, steady and healing for so long that my legs grew tired. When I finally shifted my position, he loosened his grip but didn't let me go.

"Before, when we were in the tarnished encampment, you said you'd had stupider ideas. What did you mean?" he asked.

My stomach twisted into a knot. Despite his strength keeping me up, it felt as if I'd fall to the ground. So I gave in and gently pulled away and plopped down on the ground, dress and all. We should have found a corner with a bench.

He sat beside me, and I said, "You'll ruin your suit."

"You'll ruin your dress."

"Fair point." I took a deep, steadying breath and used it to

137

brace myself. "I would say going to Chardonia in the first place, but I don't regret that. Helping people who needed it so desperately was the right thing to do. No, the real reason is I've never told anyone this before, you know."

He wrapped an arm around my shivering body. "Yet it feels like you need to let it out."

I didn't want him to be right; it was much simpler to keep things bottled up. It clearly was what was needed, though.

I told my story with a steadier voice than I thought—only a waver here and there, with his arm to support me. "I trained, you know, after I went to Chardonia and before I was tarnished. It only felt natural to fight when there was a battle against the Grand Chancellor. He held so much power over the people. It seemed like we had more supporters, but he had enough strong people on his side, mixed with that power, that nothing could stand against him. We tried anyway.

"The battle was fierce, spells flying about, stronger and far more gruesome than one of my mother's balls. People were dying everywhere, and I was trying my best to help. I became more brazen than I should have and got separated from the group. The fighting was so intense, I didn't notice until it was too late. I don't know if they cared I wasn't from Chardonia. They had to know where I came from, because as a people, we're taller and tanner than they are, but that didn't stop them from taking me prisoner and…" I couldn't finish—not even in my own head.

He pulled me closer. "I can't imagine the savageness of a person who would do that to another human being."

Without saying it, we both knew he was talking about going to the depraver. About me, and so many, *many* others getting tarnished. I shivered, and he ran a hand down my bare arm, before taking off his suit coat and draping it around me. I huddled in it, grateful that it carried his warmth and was still encased in his fresh, clean scent.

Memories assaulted me. I leaned against his shoulder and

squeezed my eyes shut against the onslaught. "It was the stupidest thing I've ever done."

"Or the bravest."

His words hit me hard. "I never thought of it like that."

"Not many people tried to take on the Grand Chancellor. He was a cruel, vicious man. Your going against him proves how good of a heart you have. How brave you are."

A strange sense of peace settled over me. "I tried. After I was tarnished, I was a slave in the Grand Chancellor's household. I hid who I was so they couldn't use me against my parents, so he never knew. When he was finally killed, I led the other tarnished out of that horrid place, and found places for us all to go. I tried to assist with their emotional wounds, but sometimes it wasn't enough."

He kissed the top of my head. "From what I heard, you did a lot of good, helping out the tarnished over there."

"I did what anyone would."

"Not true. Nobody spent more time than you, helping the tarnished figure their way back into society. Even here, we heard of how tirelessly you worked with them."

"Until Mother insisted I come home." She and I had exchanged many notes, before she finally realized I wouldn't come home on my own, and sent an escort of guards for me.

"What was it like when they tarnished you? It's not something you have to answer if you don't like."

My throat tightened, and the black markings on my skin burned. I didn't want to talk about it, but I found the words flowing out of me, like a river through a broken dam. "*Terrifying* is the best word to describe it. There was pain, yes. The depraver made certain of that. But it wasn't just the physical pain. He brutalized me with his magic. Those hours I spent screaming and fighting against him only made his grin wider and him more determined to ink me with an unalterable spell and kill my hair follicles with something similar. There's nothing left to heal, which leaves witches and warlocks everywhere baffled as to how to fix it. He marked me forever, but it wasn't just the markings. It was the grinding me down into something less than I was.

"By the time he got to making me barren, I was a wild, injured animal, lashing out at everything that came at me. He finally hit me with a knockout spell, and when I woke, it was to nothing but pain, on a cold, hard floor, left as though I really was worth less than a shadow."

His other arm came up around me, so he completely embraced me. My cheeks were wet with tears. Lots of them. No one had ever given me a chance to grieve for what I lost. I'd helped others through the process but never let myself do the same. With Lonvar holding me, I felt safe and protected. Nothing could change what happened to me, yet letting it out was cleansing.

When I was more in control of myself, I said, "Thank you for being here. I needed that."

"Anytime. I love you more deeply than I thought I could ever feel. Whatever you need, I'm here."

A rush of warmth infused me, mingled with surprise. "I love you too."

The moment was more than I ever thought I would get. It was peaceful and full of hope—until the ugly truth hit me. "I'll never be able to have children." That could change his feelings for me. I didn't want to bring it up—not yet—but I needed to make certain he knew what he was getting into with me, if we continued down this path.

"I can't imagine how painful it is, to have someone take that choice away." His voice was soft and soothing, but I couldn't be calmed.

"It was horrendous. Words can't describe it, but... That is to say..." This was far harder to talk about than I'd suspected. Yet I had to get it out. "I know we're not even together, and we still have a long way to go, before we decide—you know—*anything*, but it's important that you understand that *if* we do move forward with this relationship and someday take it all the way to marriage... Well, there will be no children." My voice cracked, betraying all the emotions scurrying inside me and trying to find a way to hide from the pain.

"Perhaps not in the traditional sense, but there are other options." He pulled away, to look me in the eye. "But I promise you that, should we continue to court until marriage, I would be the happiest man, to have you by my side."

The tension knotted in my chest eased. "Do you mean that?"

"I do."

I let myself relax back into his embrace. "Good. Though that's far in the future, if ever. I might just decide I like some other good-looking fellow who makes my heart patter."

"It's possible."

But not probable.

CHAPTER 22

The next day, I was worn and stressed. My feelings from yesterday had taken a hard toll on me, but I wouldn't change having them. I let a smile cross my face. There was still much to do, but at least I'd have Lonvar at my side.

"Better wipe the silly grin off your face, sis," Rumam said. "Here comes Mother, and she looks like she's on a rampage."

My back stiffened, and I put on a blank expression. "Thank you."

He nodded and dug into his breakfast beside me, except it was more like a late lunch. I should speak with him about the tarnished. I was positive he wasn't behind the tarnished kidnappings and killings, and he might have thoughts on what to do. So many tarnished were running out of time. Even if the public opinion was changing, it would take a while before the request for magic slowed. Many tarnished could die in that time.

Today, I would make a bigger stand. Last night's call to act should help cut down on the requests for magic and increase positive awareness of the tarnished. I'd talk to my brothers and convince them to help me hunt down whoever was behind this. It would be a busy day. I dug into my bowl of mush with gusto. I'd need my strength.

"Tawny, I would speak with you." Mother sounded as if she bit a lemon.

Across from me, Herni kept his gaze steady on the situation, but Dad couldn't seem to decide if I, Mother, or his plate was more interesting. Finally, Dad said, "It's early yet, Brundi. Let's enjoy a family breakfast."

"I won't have it. Tawny can speak with me alone or be humiliated in front of all of you."

I straightened my back and held my head high. "Nothing you can say will humiliate me ever again, Mother."

Her cheeks tinged pink, but even they wouldn't dare go red on her. "Very well. In front of the family it will be." She snapped her fingers, and the few servants who were around the room left and closed the doors behind them.

She waited a moment, probably to make sure they weren't lingering, and then cast a soundproof dome around us, in a sharp purple. "Tawny, you are a disgrace to this family and to all who look to us to lead. If you don't accept my way of doing things, I will banish you, not just from the royal house, but also from the country. If you want to act like a Chardonian *tarnished*, then you can go crawling back to them."

The way she said *tarnished* made goose bumps scatter over my arms. "I didn't know you hated people like me so much."

"Don't be ridiculous, Tawny. I don't hate them. I simply want them gone from the country, and where they can't destroy our image."

A dark, tangled feeling crept into my stomach and blossomed through my chest. "Mother, what are you saying?"

She swept her long, dark hair over her shoulder with a flick of her wrist. "You either try to be one of us, or you can go."

"No, not that part. I got that." And shockingly, it didn't hurt nearly as much as it should. "I meant the part about the tarnished."

She gave one of her dainty sniffs. "You know very well what I mean."

Pieces clicked together, as I slowly stood, my brothers surprisingly joining me. I wished there was time to choose my words carefully, but I was all too aware of how little time some had left. "Mother, have you been kidnapping the tarnished?"

Dad gasped.

Rumam turned sharp eyes on her, mouth agape with shock.

Herni's expression became sorrowful and hurt.

My hands twitched. Did I need to prepare a spell?

"Why would you say something so silly?" she responded.

I rubbed my fingers together, warming them up, just in case. "You said you knew tarnished are being kidnapped and killed for their magic. Yet, all this time, you've never done anything about it. You tried to convince me not to do anything about it, and wanted me to hide who I am. I knew it had to be someone in court. Someone high up. I just didn't think it would be you, but it has to be."

Too many things happened at once. Rumam shot Mother a look of revulsion. Herni took a step toward her, hands up like he was going to cast a spell. I brought my hand up. Mother pursed her lips. And Dad...

Poor Dad, who was married to a monstrous person willing to harm people, said, "You know about that, dearest?"

"I found out ab—" Wait. He spoke as if *he* knew about it. I slowly turned toward him. "Have you been fighting Mother on what she's been doing to the tarnished?"

"I..." He opened and closed his mouth several times, but nothing came out.

As Mother's sharp laugh echoed inside our bubble, my stomach lurched to the floor. "Daddy?"

He looked down. "I wanted your mother to be happy."

My breath came out ragged. "*You* did this?"

He jumped to his feet, but I couldn't bring myself to point my hand at him, instead keeping it trained on my mother. She was the real problem. She had to be. If it was any other way—

Dad hurried to me, tears in his eyes and streaming down his

face. I'd never seen my dad cry before. It was enough to unhinge the last vestiges of calmness.

"I'm sorry, sweetheart," he said, as he reached toward me. "I didn't know you were going to turn into a tarnished. I started this before you even left for Chardonia."

"But people are being murdered." The situation still refused to make sense in my head.

"I didn't know they were people, until you came home as a tarnished." He reached out for me.

I shook him off. "You didn't know they were people?" My voice rose without my telling it to. "How could you not know they are people? They're just like me. They are human."

He curled in on himself like a frightened animal, sobbing. "I didn't know. I swear I didn't."

"Even if I believed you, which I don't, why didn't you stop when I returned?"

"I thought about it, but I needed to keep the flow of magic coming to court. Your mother was already upset about your state. I couldn't go disappointing her and have the state of court diminish its grandeur, too."

I forced myself to blink, but when I opened my eyes, the situation still swam before me in a pool of dismay. "Daddy, how could you?"

"I just want everyone to be happy."

A dam broke loose inside me. "*Happy?* You want everyone to be *happy?* What about those whose lives you're taking? Those who've already been through so much, and now have to deal with more devastation at your hands? I've got news for you. No one is happy."

CHAPTER 23

Except for my dad's pitiful noises, stunned silence filled the room.

I couldn't bring myself to feel sorrow for him. Not one bit. He'd brought this horror down on hundreds, maybe thousands, of people. He deserved every twist of pain he got.

Once my temper was mostly under control, I turned toward my mother, who kept her expression carefully blank, like she'd taught me to do. The expression of a queen.

"Mother, we have to stop this. Today," I said.

"Oh darling, I don't think so. Once you acquiesce to my demands, court will be wanting all their spells again. We can't rightly deprive them of their magic now, can we?"

My brothers looked as aghast as I felt. "But didn't you hear what he's been doing? That he's been doing it for years? Your thirst for magic has cost lives."

"I know." The words were so plainly stated, I couldn't help but stare.

Dad didn't have the same problem. His voice hoarse, he said, "How long have you known?"

"From the moment you had the first tarnished kidnapped. I'm the queen. Nothing escapes my notice."

146

"But you never said anything." Dad sounded lost, so very lost. "I did it for you, but you never said a word."

"Well, I didn't want you to think you'd done enough, now did I?" Mother's superior mask made me blanch.

My parents were sick, sick people.

As my brothers looked as green as I felt, I said, "We're going to have to make some changes."

"I'm glad you're finally seeing things my way." Mother's smile made me shiver.

Slowly, I shook my head. "I don't think you understand. We're making some changes with how the government is run. More specifically, with who runs it."

"You wouldn't dare." Her voice went low.

"If she doesn't, I will," Rumam said.

Herni added, "As will I."

The laugh she let out made me raise my hands again, defensively.

"Oh, you silly children. Mother knows best, and that's what we're going to deal with here, before I let the sound circle down. Boys, you will follow my orders and in my footsteps. Rumam will marry Hula as I've laid out. She will continue to support me with the tarnished. Herni, I will find you someone similarly suitable. Tawny, you will stop this tarnished parading about. Everyone will do as I command."

Wait. Hula was on her side? The woman I'd gotten a faraway glance at, that was Hula. I peeked at Rumam, whose face was pale. I knew she was no good for him. Despite Mother's words, Rumam and Herni didn't move. I trembled but was left with some comfort that my brothers were on my side. "Not anymore," I said.

Her spell came flying at me, a vivid pink. I slammed down on the floor, thankful the carpet was thick.

She stalked toward me, and my brothers moved forward. Lights flashed across the room, meaning to harm or stop as the spells darted everywhere.

Someone I cared about was going to get hurt.

I rolled to the balls of my feet but kept crouched. There had to be a way to get this to stop. Dad stood off to the side, watching with growing horror on his face. He was of no use to me, but my brothers were fighting Mother with a ferocity that surprised me.

The whipping of spells flooded the room with an angry rainbow of colors. Mother laughed, and my brothers took a step back. Whatever her game, she had probably been boosted with magic from my dad's planning, whether he knew it or not. If she continued to attack with magic, we would lose. There needed to be another way to win this.

Her back was toward me, but if I sent a spell, the light would catch her attention. No, I needed to be swift and silent. My brothers were sweating under the broad range of spells. They wouldn't last much longer.

I flicked my hand out, shooting a vibrant-green spell that should freeze her.

She must have sensed it coming, because she ducked and it hurtled past. She twirled around, almost like she was dancing at a ball, but there was nothing serene or beautiful about her now.

Her face twisted in rage, fury trembling through her every action.

My brothers leapt up at the same time, but she flung a hand back at them, and with a shot of angry purple, they went flying back. Her gaze stayed focused on me, her eyes dark with the ugly passion that gripped her.

"You," she spat out. "Stupid child, can't leave well enough alone."

She stalked toward me. Another spell—a bright violet—was flung toward my head.

I ducked and rolled away from it, almost hearing it whistle past my head, except for the fact that spells were silent.

"You've always been a spoiled brat, taking your father's attention away from me. I should have gotten rid of you the moment I saw your inked face. Your meaningless life transformed into nothing, but I listened to your father, who tried to coax you along, to be one of us. You will *never* be one of us. You are worth less than a bug I'd squash under my shoe."

The horror of what she said hit me square in the chest at the same time as a spell slammed into my left shoulder and knocked me to the ground.

I was helpless, as I fought against the paralysis. She'd used my own body against me, sending it into a state where I couldn't move. Couldn't act. Could only think about her crushing words.

My own mother thought I was nothing.

Ideas were jumbled in my head, racing around each other and seeking something to grab on to. Flashing, multicolored lights surged through the air, barely missing me. Muffled sounds in the distance—my brothers fighting her.

And yet, I lay here, frozen.

I didn't even try to move, her words having done more damage than any spell could. It was one thing to know what other people thought of me, but my own mother? My stomach revolted, but still I remained stuck in place, unable to do anything but repeat her words in my head.

I was worth less than a bug, squashed under her shoe.

One of my brothers cried out. Herni, I suspected. His pain echoed through the room, mirroring that in my chest. Rumam gave a cry of fury.

They would take care of each other.

But then, he yelped in agony too.

I shifted my gaze toward them, surprised when I managed to move my eyes. My brothers were inching backward—Rumam in front of Herni, to protect him with his body, and Herni throwing out spells, doing the same for Rumam but with his magic.

Only, my mother was stalking forward like their spells were annoying gnats. My brothers were going to be back under her control. And why shouldn't they? I was less than a bug. I deserved to be squashed underfoot. Worst of all, I wasn't one of them. I wasn't part of the family or what she wanted of me.

But I knew better.

She might despise what I'd become, but I'd found a strength she'd never know. Even if she hated me and wished to mold me back into a vain girl who barely thought of others, there was more to me. I was tarnished, yes, but it was also mine to defy her expectations of anguish.

I would not let her win the battle or the war.

Quiet as I could, I jumped to my feet, grabbed a pot of mush, and crept over toward her. She started to turn, but before she could come at me, I slammed the pot onto her head as hard as I could.

Sticky cereal flew everywhere. It was a mess, like a food fight, but far more dangerous. Mother crumpled, but I caught her before she dropped to the floor, grateful to see she was alive. As much as I wanted this to be over, I didn't want to kill her.

I plopped down, settling her onto my lap. My voice came out flat, when I said, "Get help."

The sound circle was gone, and so was any protection I'd had from my parents.

CHAPTER 24

The guards rushed in, and Mila was among them.

It took a lot of explaining to get them to process why the queen was out cold, and that I'd been the one to do it.

"Look," Rumam said to the head guard. "My mother is a danger not only to us, but also to the whole country. We need to have her locked up."

"I can't throw the queen in a cell." The man's expression was aghast.

Dad stood from where he'd slumped into a chair and straightened to his full height. "You will, and you'll throw me in, too."

Mila shot a look at me, but then turned her attention back to her duty with a nod.

My heart gave a painful squeeze at Dad's words, but I didn't show the wince I wanted to. Dad was right. They both needed to be where they couldn't do any more harm.

"But the queen has the final say. If she was awake, she wouldn't agree to this." The guard put a hand to his hip, where his gun sat.

I tensed, but Herni surprised me by saying, "The queen doesn't always have the final say. Under the Code of Conduct, in Section Five, Paragraph Forty-three, it states that if the heir to the throne can

151

prove beyond doubt that the ruling monarch is harming the country and the people therein, that monarch will be discharged from their position, and the next in line for the throne will take their place."

We all stared at him. No one read the Code of Conduct, let alone memorized it. It was far too monotonous.

"Does it really say that?" I asked.

He nodded. "We can pull out a copy if you'd like, but it's quite clear."

"Forgive me, Prince Herni," the head guard said, "but wouldn't that mean the heir could say the monarch is harming people and get the crown for themselves?"

"No. You must show proof beyond doubt. I believe our sister has that." Herni looked to me.

Wait. Me? I didn't have anything. Except perhaps— "The queen had knowledge of the king's enslaving and killing tarnished refugees, and not only permitted it, but also encouraged it. I know someone who can show us the encampments. Mila will back me up on this."

She nodded. "I've been there. We'll get the information for you."

"Don't bother," Dad said. "I will tell you where every single one is located, and I will give you anything else you need, to take my wife and me far away and strip us of our power to rule. Apparently, it's necessary." He looked down at Mother, his face twisted in an agony I understood, in part.

The guards exchanged looks. Mila stayed close to me. Everyone looked lost.

I didn't blame the others; I felt rather adrift myself. Perhaps there was something I could do. "Rumam should be placed as regent, until we can get this sorted. I'm certain Herni can find a way to make that happen."

Herni nodded, but Rumam paled. "I'm not ready."

"Ready or not, we have to do something." I hurried to him and put an arm around him. "Besides, I believe in you."

He didn't get his color back, but he did smile faintly. "And here I thought my little sister didn't like me."

I let an impish grin spread across my lips. "Who said I like you? Believing and liking are two entirely different things."

He gave a soft chuckle, but his mirth didn't last long. We might want to try for levity, but the situation was far heavier than laughter could cut through.

"To start, let's get the queen and king bound so their magic can't be used. And quickly, before she wakes." Rumam didn't wait for the guards to move, but bent down over Mother himself and threw her over his shoulder.

I always believed he was strong, but the movement still surprised me.

"Let's go," he said, looking at Dad.

Dad said, "I promise I will be there in one moment. I need to make apologies to your sister."

"Make it quick." Rumam ordered two of the guards to remain with us, and Mila insisted on staying as well, but the rest went with him, Mother, and Herni.

Mila and the other guards backed up so that we wouldn't be heard if we spoke low, but close enough that she could move in if needed.

I gave her a grateful smile and shifted my weight, uncertain what to think, say, or do. That my dad had been involved in all of this— No, not involved. He *instigated* this, and it left so vast a torrent of emotions in me, I couldn't seem to grab on to any one of them.

"I'm sorry," he said after a long pause.

Looking up at him through the blur of tears, I said, "I'm not sure I can forgive you. Not right away."

"I understand, and I will take your forgiveness when I can earn it. I… I wasn't thinking about the things I should have, when I began having the tarnished taken. Everything I can say is an excuse, but mostly, I wanted everyone to be happy. I see now not only how very wrong I was, but also that it never mattered what I did. Your mother would never have been happy."

"I wish it wasn't so, but I understand about wanting to do what she asks and keep her appeased. But it's obvious you still care more about her than the lives lost for her vanity."

"I'm sorry." His eyes were downcast. "I will have to relearn how to value what's truly important."

That was an understatement.

He held out a hand toward me, but pulled it back. Just as well. I wasn't ready to accept his embrace and didn't know whether I ever would be.

"Don't forget that, despite all my faults, I love you, Tawny. I'll be working to repair the damage I've done." He didn't let me have a chance to respond as he strode out the door, guards with him.

CHAPTER 25

Envado reacted surprisingly well to the shift of power to Rumam. Once my father told us where to find all the information we needed, things progressed quickly. Some people still acted against the tarnished, but my doing official royal duties in public as a tarnished seemed to sway opinion to their side.

I just couldn't believe my dork of a brother was king.

Mother had been forcibly taken to a well-guarded house in the countryside that was specifically set up to not let her use her magic. I didn't know whether or not I wanted Dad to join her, but thankfully it wasn't up to me. He asked Rumam to send him.

Dad was under the same restrictions as Mother. He sent me and my brothers letters often, and tried to make amends for his actions. Besides giving us all he knew, he donated all of her personal items, such as clothing and baubles, to be sold for those in need. He wrote letters of apology to the tarnished and court. I still hadn't forgiven him, despite it being several months, but I was close. At least I had my brothers, Mila, and Lonvar to help me through it all.

Rumam had made changes to allow more compassion for those in need, whether tarnished or not. The refugees were welcome to live where they wanted and assisted in finding work that would suit them. Anyone caught treating them as less than a human was taken and tried according to what they had done.

Those involved in the scheme against the tarnished had been imprisoned and only let out under guard to do service for the community. They helped build houses and furniture for the tarnished, worked in vegetable gardens and ranches to help provide food for those in need. Though they would have to prove themselves trustworthy in order to do so.

Hula, though, she'd been a sore spot for Rumam. She'd been sent to prison, not given any special treatment even though she was a member of court. Rumam had seen to that, and the same for any other member of court Dad said had been aiding in the plot to steal magic from the tarnished.

"Heavy thoughts, sis?" Rumam asked, making me jump from my seat in the garden.

Mila stood guard nearby, out of sight but a steady presence in my life that I probably took far too much for granted.

Fall had come, leaving me with a thick cloak and gloves, but I kept my head bare despite the warmth leeching out of me. "They seem to be growing lighter every day, but sometimes I can't help but dwell on our previously hidden reality."

"I understand." He sat by me on the bench, his shoulders slumping.

I kept my voice soft. "I'm sorry about Hula."

He waved me away. "I know you didn't like her."

"How?"

"Trust me, sis, you didn't do a good job of hiding it even with your royal training."

Heat flushed through my face. "Sorry."

"Don't be. You were right to dislike her. I should have realized there was a reason Mother had been pushing the two of us together so much, but all I wanted to see was the attention Hula paid to me." He sighed. "I never loved her or anything, but it still hurts a man's pride."

"I'm sorry you were hurt."

"Me too, but it wasn't near as much as some." He frowned before his expression lightened. "At least things are getting better."

"Yes, King Rumam," I teased, and hoped I didn't push too much with my next words. "Now instead of half the unmarried women in the country wanting to be your wife, they all do."

He laughed, the twinkle returning to his eyes instead of the pain. "Can't say I'm shooing them away. Though there's a certain young man I probably should shoo away from you."

Heat seared my cheeks. "Lonvar is a good man." And an even better kisser.

Rumam laughed. "That doesn't mean I'm ready to let him marry my sister."

"There's no talk of that. Not yet." My face grew hotter.

"It'll come." He sombered. "I'm sorry I wasn't there for you more, growing up and when you were tarnished. I can't imagine how hard it must have been. I should have come to Chardonia."

"You didn't even know if I was alive then."

"Well, not until later, but I should have come as soon as I knew."

"You were there when it mattered," I said.

He shook his head. "I'll let you think so, but I'll always wish I'd done things differently. You should never have been tarnished."

How different would my life have been? "I wouldn't go back and change the fact that it happened, as horrid as it was." Though I could think of it with less shuddering than I used to. "It's made me the person I am now. I didn't understand the true value of others until more recently—or even my own value. Though, I would never have accepted people dying for magic, but more than just that changed after I left. I was lucky that my restlessness and seeing my friends help Chardonia made me want to go. Being tarnished was a part of that, horrid or not."

"You've grown."

"More than you have," I teased again.

He sat straighter. "Someone needs to bring levity to the monarchy, after what this country has been through."

"And you're the perfect man for the job."

"I don't know about that, but I do my best." He shrugged.

His best was better than he thought. "Why were you always gone when I was younger?" I asked.

"Lots of reasons. Mother sent us out often, so I could learn about ruling, and I liked to take Herni with me as company. After a while, I realized I liked being away from the pressures coming from court and Mother, so I went as often as I could. I should have realized it would affect my ability to see things I needed to, concerning the country, Chardonia, and you."

"I understand. Mother's demands were… a lot to deal with."

"Doesn't excuse me, but I'm glad I'm not the only one who thought so." His smile started off sad but quickly turned mischievous. "I forgot to tell you, Lonvar is here."

I snorted. "More like you purposefully kept the information from me."

He stood and said, "I'll send him over, but he'd better stay standing. That bench is small."

I laughed. "Your Majesty must have a big bottom, then."

With a wave, he said, "Thank you for all you've done, Tawny. We wouldn't have known about what was happening if you hadn't told us."

"I only relayed what Lonvar told me."

"It was more than that, and we both know it."

It was an old argument, ever since he'd become king.

I said, "There's still much to do."

"There always is." With a nod, he left.

Only moments later, Lonvar strode around the bushes. He must not have been far.

I grinned and wrapped him in a hug.

He pressed a long, steady kiss to my lips in response.

I shivered with pleasure at being so near him.

After what my brothers would have deemed far too long, we

broke apart and made it back to the bench I'd been sitting on. I made sure to scoot close to him, in case my brothers happened by. And because I wanted to.

"How was work today?" I asked. He spent most of the day working as a law officer, determined to help put things back to the order and justice they should have been in the first place. I hadn't seen much of him as of late.

"Better now that I'm with you," he said.

"You're full of flattery today."

He chuckled. "It was good. We finished rounding up the last of those who worked against the tarnished."

"I didn't think you'd ever get them all."

"They snitched each out, once they realized how serious we were and that they no longer had royal sanction. Most were in it for the money—those were the easy ones to catch—but we've finally found the ones intent on harming the tarnished." He wrapped an arm around me and pulled me even closer.

"I'm grateful to have them off the streets. So many tarnished have been pulled through far too much, but that's finally easing." I rested my head on his shoulder.

"Because you're doing so much good work with them."

"Only doing what anyone would in my situation."

"Not everyone would put themselves at such risk for others. You freed that woman you spoke with and all others in that encampment yourself. You've been working with the tarnished, your brothers, and anyone willing to help, to make a better place in the world for everyone."

He was right. I could have easily done what my mother wanted, to hide my tarnished state by frivolously using my magic. "I'm trying my best and have finally decided that's good enough."

"More than." He pressed a kiss to my head. "You're freezing. We should go inside."

"It's a good excuse to stay close to you." Not that I needed one. "Thank you for coming to me all those months ago and bringing

159

to me see the tarnished. I know you were only doing your job, but it turned into so much more. For me, at least."

"For me too."

I did still have questions I wanted answers to. "Why did you think it was Rumam behind the plot?"

"Our information from someone that had worked at one of the camps, knew Hula, and told us about her. He said the plot came from the royal family, likely the Crown Prince. We assumed it was correct, based on other things we heard about the tarnished being taken. Whoever was behind the plot had to hold enough power to cover it for so long."

"Makes sense. Likely it was one of my parents trying to cover their tracks." It made me sad, but I would come to terms with it as I slowly came to understand the rest. "I wish things had turned out different, but I'm glad we're finally making progress."

"I am, as well."

I bit my lip.

"Whatever it is, you can ask me. I won't hold back anything more from you. All of my secrets are yours."

The thought had me leaning in closer. "When we were going to pose me as one of the captured tarnished, who did you talk to, in the alleyway?"

"I went to my boss's house. She lives in the basement there. I let her know where we were going and what we were doing. She protested, of course, but only half-heartedly. She could see the value of what we were going to do, probably better than I did. Best of all, she promised to bring a group in to save us, if needed."

"I'm glad we had that, even if I didn't know it. And before you protest, I know why you didn't tell me. I wish you would have—that you could have—but we've all had to make hard choices these past months. You did what you thought was best, even if I wished otherwise." We sat silent for several moments, before I leaned my forehead against him with a sigh.

I wanted to keep the peace of the moment, but— "I have duties I should get to."

"Mila would prefer you to stay in the garden with me. Easier to protect that way."

I laughed. "I believe that's your preference, not hers."

"You've got me there." He pulled me into an embrace.

"I love you."

"I love you too, Tawny."

I brushed my lips against his—once, twice, and then a third time. I deepened the kiss. Love, caring, and peace flowed out of me through my lips and into him.

He cupped his hand on the back of my head, keeping me in place. I ran my fingers through his hair and down his neck.

He was so close. Not just physically, but also where I could share my heart with him.

When we finally broke apart, I was breathless but wanting more. I snuck another peck and drew back, to see him wholly focused on me.

He said, "Asking you to dance was the best thing I have ever done."

"Accepting your request was the best thing *I've* ever done." I curled up against his side. "Are you still free to help me teach the tarnished tomorrow?" I had been taking time every day, to teach classes and provide groups on coming together with those who'd gone through the same trials, working through their feelings, and how to find their place in society. All for the tarnished refugees who struggled with all that they had gone through. The classes were going well, with lots of participation. People were healing. Lonvar joined me when he could, along with many other Envadi who wanted to assist. "I'll be there," he said.

"Thank you."

"It's my pleasure."

As we snuggled close and I thought of those I would help tomorrow, I was struck by how well this was working. Lonvar and I weren't the only ones helping the refugees and the country come together. Tarnished or not, there were many coming forward to help. Envado was healing from the damage my own

161

parents had wrought. It would take time to continue to get better, but people were headed in the right direction. Much had changed, and I'd never felt brighter.

Even spells had nothing on how I felt now. The gleam of magic when I cast spells for my appearance had been breathtaking, but when I looked in the mirror now, it was all mine. Mine to burn bright and give hope to a nation.

The End

Discover the start of what happened in Chardonia with the Grand Chancellor in You Are Mine, book one in the complete Mine series.
https://books2read.com/u/bw7gKP

Janeal's Newsletter
https://landing.mailerlite.com/webforms/landing/g8l6j7

ABOUT THE AUTHOR

Janeal Falor has published over twenty novels including the Mine series, Death's Queen, and Sands of Eppla. She lives in Utah with her husband and three children. In her non-writing time she teaches her kids to make silly faces, cooks whatever strikes her fancy, and attempts to cultivate a garden even when half the things she plants die. When it's time for a break she can be found taking a scenic drive with her family or drinking hot chocolate.

http://janealfalor.com

www.ingramcontent.com/pod-product-compliance
Lightning Source LLC
Chambersburg PA
CBHW070552180626
46817CB00005B/1798